They had a view of the moon-silvered sand of the curving beach. It was low tide. Out in the sea, the fringing coral had emerged, glistening wetly in the weak, celestial light.

"And another thing you know about me," Leslie continued, "is that I'm in love with you."

Before Julie had a chance to say a word, he crushed her against him and she felt the warmth of his lips on hers. The pleasant shock of his kiss drove all other thoughts from her mind. She relaxed in his arms, lulled by his embrace.

Dear Readers:

Thank you for your unflagging interest in First Love From Silhouette. Your many helpful letters have shown us that you have appreciated growing and stretching with us, and that you demand more from your reading than happy endings and conventional love stories. In the months to come we will make sure that our stories go on providing the variety you have come to expect from us. We think you will enjoy our unusual plot twists and unpredictable characters who will surprise and delight you without straying too far from the concerns that are very much part of all our daily lives.

We hope you will continue to share with us your ideas about how to keep our books your very First Loves. We depend on you to keep us on our toes!

Nancy Jackson
Senior Editor
FIRST LOVE FROM SILHOUETTE

A Blossom Valley Book

CORAL ISLAND
Elaine Harper

Published by Silhouette Books New York
America's Publisher of Contemporary Romance

First Love from Silhouette

Though the setting Coral Island is based on a real island, the name is fictitious. All other geographical references in this book are authentic.

SILHOUETTE BOOKS
300 E. 42nd St., New York, N.Y. 10017

Copyright © 1986 by Emily Hallin

ISBN: 0-373-06197-8

First Silhouette Books printing August 1986

America's Publisher of Contemporary Romance

Printed in the U.S.A.

RL 6.6, IL age 11 and up

Read **Coral Island**
Seventeenth of the **Blossom Valley books**
And these other Blossom Valley books
by
Elaine Harper

ELAINE HARPER grew up in Colorado, and later went to high school and college in Missouri. After her marriage she moved to California. She now lives in a town very much like Blossom Valley. For some years she worked at Stanford University. Her constant association with the students inspired her to write young adult fiction.

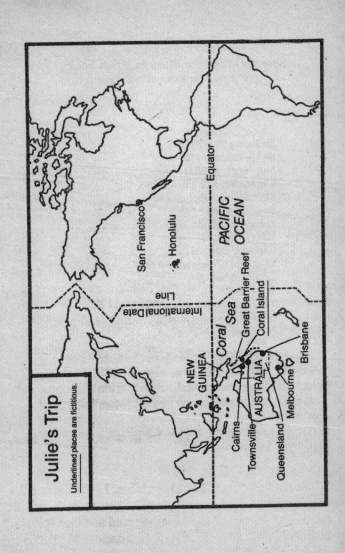

Julie's Trip

Underlined places are fictitious.

San Francisco

Honolulu

PACIFIC OCEAN

Equator

International Date Line

NEW GUINEA

Coral Sea

Great Barrier Reef

Coral Island

Cairns

Townsville

Queensland

AUSTRALIA

Melbourne

Brisbane

Chapter One

You've heard that old saying, 'When it rains, it pours,'" Julie Blacker commented to her friend Kim. "Well, that applies to my whole junior year, and it's ending up with a cloudburst!"

"Aren't you being pessimistic? What's so bad?"

"Bad! It's a disaster! You know that this whole year I've been waiting for Mike to come home from Oregon State."

"I have heard you use the phrase, 'when Mike gets back,' a few jillion times."

"Then you know what could be the worst thing that could happen to me."

"It's something about Mike."

"Something devastating about Mike. I called over at his house to find out exactly when he was getting back, and his mom sort of hemmed and hawed around and then said that he'd be delayed a few weeks. He had decided to bike up to

Canada with some of his college friends. What do you want to bet that one of them is of the opposite sex?"

"You don't know that, do you? You're just blowing this up. I told you you should try to date other guys while Mike was away at college. If you had accepted my advice, you wouldn't be taking this so hard."

It was too much for Julie's friend to criticize her, when she was already down. She made an excuse to terminate the telephone conversation, and just sat there at the phone bench thinking things over.

When had all this happened? Julie reflected that Mike's letters had been few and far between in recent months. She took them out of the enameled box with a butterfly on top and read them over. At first, all he could write about was how homesick he was, and how he had missed her. The latest letters were much more impersonal. Now that she analyzed them, they were mere token answers to her eager letters to him. Not once had he mentioned that he was looking forward to the summer and seeing her. The whole thing was clear. He had lost interest. He had another girlfriend. She'd been dumped! Soon her rejection would be common knowledge around Blossom Valley. Kim had reminded her how often she'd referred to the time when Mike would return. Everyone in town would remember that, and now they were going to find out he wasn't coming and she would be humiliated. Her conversation with Kim had proved the point.

From that moment Julie began to avoid her friends for fear they would tease her about it. She even hid out from her family. She didn't want them to know she'd been wrong about Mike, that he had betrayed her.

"I'm not hungry," she said one night when she decided to skip dinner.

"Are you sick?" her mother asked.

"Don't I have the privilege of not feeling like eating?" When her mother left, Julie put out a Do Not Disturb sign on her door and stayed in her room feeling miserable.

She realized that she shouldn't have expected Mike to stay faithful to her when he went to college. It would be so easy to forget a totally ordinary person with a moon face and plain, short brown hair. His abandonment led her to think of all the disappointments she had suffered in the past year. For instance, missing all the school parties, because she was waiting for Mike Washburn. She had tried to keep herself busy so she wouldn't miss him, but she'd been bored most of the year just writing letters to him or staring at his picture. She'd tried to get on the girls' basketball team, but she was too short. The swimming coach told her she had talent, and she had gone out for the team. She would have made it but she got fungus in her ear, and the doctor told her she had to stay out of the water for a while. She had learned to knit then, and had made Mike a pair of mittens—he said it was cold in Oregon—and now she knew he'd probably used them to hold hands with other girls. Life was unfair. Some people got everything, and others—like herself—were left with nothing. Nobody loved her.

There was a knock at her bedroom door, and when she didn't answer, the door opened.

"Didn't you see that Do Not Disturb sign?" Julie asked with a snarl.

"I thought you needed to be disturbed." Her brother, Harlan, stood commandingly in the door, his intense black eyes boring into hers. "Snap out of it, Julie. This is what they call, if I may use a cliché, 'wallowing in self-pity.' So Mike isn't coming back after school's out. Big deal!"

Julie picked up a stuffed plush turtle and hurled it at him.

"Don't you have any respect for anybody's feelings?" she shrieked. Harlan caught the turtle and sat down on the edge of Julie's bed, tossing the plush reptile up in the air and catching it.

He was maddening. He was one of Julie's problems. He was always in the limelight because he was an environmental protester. People kidded her about Harlan's fiery oratory on various causes, and sometimes referred to him as "your pinko brother."

"I have a lot of respect for my little sister, and I wish she had some for herself," he said.

"Go away."

"Come on, Julie. These things happen all the time. High school sweethearts get separated and meet other people. They drift apart. It's been happening for eons. It's part of life. You grow up by going through it."

"A lot you know. You still have your high school sweetheart. You never have been separated from Martha, and if you ever get a job, you guys will probably get married. You don't know what it's like, so don't preach to me."

"You might even get him back eventually, if you'll calm down and act like a normal human being."

"I never want to see him again. Will you kindly go away?"

"No, I won't. People who feel as bad as you do need to talk to somebody. If you don't want to talk to me, how about calling up one of your friends—like Kim?"

"She'd only make fun of me for talking all year about the great things I'd do when Mike came home. Everybody envied me last year because I dated this senior, and now they feel sorry for me. There are only two weeks of school left, and I'm not going. I can't face all those people who'll be ridiculing me about being dumped."

"Julie, get yourself together. Nobody is going to know or care. You're just exaggerating your own importance. Everyone else is concerned with his own affairs. Besides, you haven't been dumped. Mike is a college guy. He's free to take a vacation in Canada if he wants. Why don't you write and tell him to have a good time? Then go ahead and have a good summer yourself. You're a terrific kid. Give some other guy a chance to know you. You ought to feel free, instead of cooping yourself up. Now you can forget about him and get to know some interesting people you've been ignoring all year.''

"There's nobody I want to know. Will you get off my back and leave me alone? You don't know anything about rejection. All I want is some privacy.''

"I want you to go to the movies with Martha and me tonight. It's unhealthy for you to stay in here by yourself. Forget about all this.''

"And have everybody see me out with my brother, without a date! They'll put two and two together. Harlan and Martha are trying to cheer Julie up because she's been thrown overboard by Mike Washburn.''

"You are so stubborn. Okay, I'm losing my patience. If you won't let anybody help you, go ahead and enjoy your misery.'' Harlan, his eyes shooting sparks, stomped out of the room, and Julie wished he'd come back, but he didn't. She found herself looking at Mike's picture and going over his letters again, mulling over some snapshots taken when they were both in Blossom Valley High going out together, thinking it would be like this forever.

Julie's parents wouldn't let her quit school, but in the few days that remained she slipped in and out of classes, retreating from her friends, disappearing at lunch time so no one would have a chance to ask her when Mike was coming home. She continued to skip meals or pick at her food so that her family scolded her. When she didn't respond, they whispered among themselves, trying to think of something to blast her out of her moodiness.

"I think she needs a change of scene," Harlan said. "If she could go where nobody knows about her and Mike, she could get a different perspective on things. She has this ridiculous idea that everyone is concentrating on her and her problem, and she's afraid they'll bring it up."

Mrs. Blacker thought of various relatives whom Julie might visit. There was illness in Aunt Rose's family. Uncle Dick had those three small children for whom Julie would end up being a baby-sitter and a drudge. There seemed to be no place for Julie to forget her sorrow. They considered summer camp, but it was too late to enroll.

"She really doesn't have any problem at all," Mr. Blacker said in exasperation. "It's all in her mind."

"It's none the less real to her," Mrs. Blacker responded. "She'll be idle all summer and this will grow to large proportions. The rest of us have our work, we're too busy to understand. But Julie is a sensitive adolescent, who right now feels her life is ruined."

Harlan, who was listening, suddenly leaped from his chair. "Dad, you're going on a trip this summer. Take Julie with you. How could she get a better perspective on things than by going clear out of the country?"

At first Mrs. Blacker looked dubious, then slowly her face illuminated. "Why not?" she agreed. "It would be a boost to Julie's ego to junket around with her dad this summer."

"Are you two serious?" Mr. Blacker took off his spectacles and polished them, then replaced them, peering through as if to find some evidence that they were only kidding. "This is a business trip. I'll be working, attending conferences, interviewing people. I couldn't pay proper attention to Julie, to say nothing of the cost of a ticket to Australia. It's halfway around the world you know."

"But Julie is sixteen. She doesn't need to be watched over like a little child. With all the connections you'll have over there, surely she could meet some other young people to spend time with while you're busy."

"Perhaps, but the cost!" Mr. Blacker smote his head in frustration. He was a newspaperman, researching articles on business for a big daily in the city. He was going to Australia in connection with a series of feature articles he was doing on a world-wide crisis in the sugar industry, and incidentally, to pick up what other stories he could find there. His own expenses would be paid for by the paper, but such a trip for Julie would be an expensive proposition.

"I have a job out at the bird refuge," Harlan said, "so I won't be any expense."

"I could put off getting those new drapes for the house," Mrs. Blacker contributed.

"I think you two are conspiring to get Julie off your hands and onto mine," Mr. Blacker commented.

"It's not too pleasant having someone moping around you all the time," Mrs. Blacker conceded.

"But that's the whole idea. She'll quit being a drag if she has new things to do and see," Harlan said.

"I'm rather wary of this scheme," Mr. Blacker said, "but maybe it's not such a preposterous idea after all. I'll consider it."

Julie's father mulled over the prospect all week. He found that he could get a special fare for two by traveling in the middle of the week, and that accommodations in Cairns, where he'd be spending most of his time, were not too expensive. He broke the news to Julie one evening when the family was barbecuing some fish in the backyard.

"I've just been thinking, Julie," he began, "how lonely a person can be when he's traveling. Eating alone, and so forth. I might need some company when I go on that assignment to Australia, and I thought of taking you along."

Julie was electrified out of her lethargy. "Me! Go to Australia!" Then her eyes narrowed and she shot guarded glances around at the family, to see how the others were reacting. "You're putting me on. Teasing."

"On my honor, I'm serious. You're getting to be a young lady. You've never been out of California."

"I was on the Nevada side of Lake Tahoe once," Julie reminded him.

"That doesn't count," he said, laughing. "I thought this would be a good chance for you to broaden your horizons."

"But why me? Why not take Mom, if you need company? I get it, this is another plot to get me to forget about Mike."

Mr. Blacker grimaced, and then grinned. "You caught me red-handed. As for Mom, she can't go. She has a job, remember, and this is her busy season. But we have been concerned that you're taking your personal disappointment too hard."

"Amen," Harlan chimed in, arranging the barbecue coals.

"That's enough, Harlan." Mr. Blacker continued. "To be honest, one of my objectives in inviting you is to distract you from your obsession with this boy. But it's also an educational opportunity for you to see what another part of the world is like. I'd enjoy showing you around over there, and who knows? You might even find yourself having fun."

"Australia seems pretty awesome to me. You're sure you don't mind, Mom? And what about you, Harlan, being the oldest, you won't get your nose out of joint if I get to go on this trip and you don't?"

"We've all discussed this," Mrs. Blacker said. "Harlan was the one who suggested that Dad take you."

"So you've been talking about me behind my back?"

"Of course, honey. We don't like to see you unhappy. We've all been thinking of ways to bring back that laughter we haven't been hearing recently," her mother responded.

Julie had mixed emotions about the trip. In a way, it might be boring to go on a business trip with one's father, even if it was to a far-out place like Australia. But the prospect of getting into a new scene at this particular time was irresistible. The more she thought about it the more excited she became. She might see real kangaroos in the wild! She and her dad looked up articles about Australia in old *National Geographics*. "The area we'll visit is right here near the Great Barrier Reef. Maybe we can get out there," Mr. Blacker said.

Julie looked at pictures of coral and giant clams and exotic fish. She and her dad had never spent so much time together. They looked at maps and made plans. She had never dreamed of having so much in common with her rather awesome father.

"I've made contact with some people in Cairns in the sugar industry. They have two youngsters, Jane and Leslie, who are near your age, and they're eager to meet an American teenager. They want us to come out to a barbecue on the very first evening we're there."

"Neat," Julie said. The trip had pretty well pushed Mike Washburn to the back of her mind, though he still hadn't disappeared. She just didn't have much time to think about him. She had to put in a rush order for a passport, for she'd never been out of the United States before. When she saw her name and her picture in such an official document, it made her feel like some kind of VIP.

"I wonder what those girls, Jane and Leslie, are like?" Julie's friend, Kim, asked. "What do you think they wear, and what kind of amusements do they go in for? What will you do if they're impossible creeps and you have to spend all your time with them?''

"The only thing I know about them is that they barbecue, so maybe they'll be pretty much like Californians," Julie answered.

"Maybe Leslie and Jane will know some guys," Kim suggested.

"I doubt if I'll meet any guys in such a short time," Julie said. "Since I'm supposed to be keeping my dad company, I may be spending my time listening to stuffy lectures or going to banquets with a lot of stodgy businessmen or just waiting outside some office door while Dad interviews someone."

"Julie Blacker! I didn't imagine anyone could make a trip halfway around the world sound so boring! You want to trade places with me?''

"Not really. I'm curious to see what Australia and Australian kids are like. But they only invited me to a barbecue. That will probably be the last of them."

Harlan, who was a bird enthusiast, asked her to take notes on any unusual birds she saw. "But I don't know enough about birds to tell which ones are unusual!" she replied.

"Anyway, keep your eyes open. I'm glad Dad's taking you, Julie, but I'll admit I'm envious, even though you need the trip more than I do."

That remark made Julie remember the misery that led her father to invite her along, and, remembering, her eyes resumed that look of anguish. She thought about Mike biking around Canada with his new friends, and probably his new girl, and the memories of that sophomore year when he'd been her boyfriend rose to engulf her with a fear that in Australia she was only going to be homesick—a drag on her father. He'd wish he hadn't taken her.

She doubted, anyway, that she could provide him with the company he claimed to need. She watched her dad as he sat at his desk in his wire-rimmed glasses, his forehead creased with thought as he worked on his papers. What did she really know about him? Sure, he was the guy who had taken her on picnics to the beach and had bought her ice-cream cones, who played Santa Claus on Christmas, read her stories when she was a little kid and praised her for good grades when she was a bigger one. He was the one who doled out her allowance and paid the bills for her clothing and other possessions, who had taught her how to swim and shoot baskets and how to drive. He knew her well enough to have discerned her pain at Mike's abandonment and to rescue her from the humiliation it would have caused if she'd stayed in Blossom Valley all summer.

But how well did she know him? The real guy, when he wasn't at home being a dad. All she knew was that he was a reporter, and she didn't even read his stories in the newspaper because they were all about business, a boring subject to a teenager. What was she going to talk to her dad about for those weeks in a strange country? Was he going to have to amuse her and neglect his work? Would they both be sorry she had come?

Even when they were strapped into their airplane seats and were taking off for her very first long plane flight, Julie sidled a look at her father and thought he was inscrutable. He had his briefcase with him, stuffed with mysterious papers and notepads on which he made jottings that must be important and learned. Even though he was her own father whom she had seen practically every day of her life, she felt tongue-tied, knowing she couldn't carry on a conversation that would interest him for the interminable hours they would be on the plane.

There was plenty of entertainment on the flight, however, for the attendants served Cokes and nuts, and then dinner. After that there was a movie, which was hard to understand on the earphones. When that was over, Julie tried to go to sleep, although she was so cramped that she only got a catnap, wakening when she had to move an inch.

After a while they landed in Honolulu where they had to change planes, and her dad told her about other times he had been there. In fact, he and her mother had come to Honolulu back in the sixties on their honeymoon. "It wasn't as crowded then as it is now," he said. "We rented a car and went around Oahu discovering different beaches."

Julie tried to imagine her father and mother twenty years ago when they were carefree newlyweds. She had seen pictures of them at their wedding, looking very young. It was hard—in fact, impossible—to imagine a time when she and Harlan had not even been born. It gave her an eerie feeling to think of the world existing without her on it.

They boarded another airplane, had another meal, saw another movie and had another uncomfortable nap. When she woke up, her dad said, with a mischievous twinkle in his eye, "While you were asleep the 27th of June disappeared." He showed her the International Date Line on the map. "Even though our airplane has been racing the sun toward the west, we lost a day. Don't worry, though. We'll make it up on the way home."

Just before landing in Cairns, Australia, Julie decided to freshen up a little. Those girls, Jane and Leslie, were going to meet them at the plane, and they would be all freshly dressed, washed and brushed.

In the cramped lavatory, Julie tried to make herself presentable. The harsh fluorescent light made her look weird. Combing didn't do much for her hair, which she'd been sleeping on for hours, and it was standing on end. Her

complexion had a ghastly cast. Maybe it was just the light—
or could it be the spasmodic, upright naps on the plane?
Anyway, she could haunt a house.

"We're on another continent, Dad!" Julie exclaimed as
the plane touched down. Her father took her carry-on bag
from her and they proceeded into customs to get their luggage cleared, and on into the airport lobby.

Someone shouted, "That must be the Blackers!" and a
group of people advanced toward them.

Mr. Blacker said, "It's the Donaldsons." He took Julie's
elbow and propelled her toward them.

Her ears were slightly plugged and she felt lightheaded
and unreal. She looked into the welcoming faces of a middle-aged couple, a dark-haired friendly looking girl about
Julie's age, and a tall, smiling blond guy with very inquisi-
tive gray eyes.

"So you're Julie!" he exclaimed, grasping both her hands
in his. "I'm Leslie, and this is Jane." He said Jane as if it
were spelled "Jine," reminding Julie that she was in a foreign country.

Chapter Two

We'll take you right over to the house," Mrs. Donaldson said. "I know you must be tired, and you can just relax there."

"We ought to go to the hotel, leave our luggage and clean up a bit," Julie was glad to hear her father say. Under the close scrutiny of this attractive guy, Leslie, she felt disheveled and gritty-eyed. Her tongue felt dry and her skin drawn. After all, she had been strapped for seventeen hours in a cramped airplane seat. She desperately wanted to take a shower and sleep around the clock.

"Nonsense! You can make yourselves at home at our place," Mrs. Donaldson said. "Clean up there. Jane and Leslie have been so impatient to meet Julie. They've never known an American girl before."

Julie was dismayed at this news. They were expecting her to sparkle and shine and be amusing. She gave the young Donaldsons a ghost of a smile. It was enough of a shock to find that Leslie was a guy—a vigorous, energetic, handsome one—and that he was seeing her at her worst. He was so close to her that he could look right down on her rumpled head.

"Just consider my room yours," Jane insisted. "Anything you need, just ask."

"Feel free to take a shower while we're organizing the barbecue," Mrs. Donaldson added.

Julie felt her head swimming. She exchanged a sympathetic glance with her dad. They watched while their suitcases and tote bags were stowed in the trunk of the Donaldson's car. Mr. Blacker got in front with Mr. and Mrs. Donaldson and Julie was squeezed in the middle of the back seat, the target of Jane and Leslie's curiosity. There was hardly room for Leslie's broad shoulders, so he put his arm around the back of the seat to fit in, and eventually, his hand came to rest on Julie's shoulder. This had the effect of scrunching her up against him. Julie didn't want to be that close when she felt so unattractive. She found herself stiffening and freezing up. The evening was going to be a disaster. Right away she was going to turn off the Donaldson kids and their friends. She'd be a drag on her dad for the whole month they were in Australia. The Donaldsons, however, didn't seem to notice how grungy she was. Jane chattered away as the car sped from the airport to their home.

"You're going to meet Katherine, my best friend, and some blokes we know, John and Richard. Leslie here hasn't got any friends coming, so you'll be stuck with him."

Julie's spirits sank still lower. More strangers were going to be appalled at the sight of the American zombie who'd just descended from the stratosphere.

"My friends are all either down at Townsville going to college or out on the reef, where I work," Leslie said, his face very near to Julie's. "But it's just as well. They might give me some competition if they were here."

"Leslie should have been going to college at Townsville this year, but he decided to put it off and work instead," Jane said.

"I had a summer job on the reef, and I enjoyed it so much that when they asked me to stay on, I thought I'd take a break from education and build up a bank account. I'll get back to school next year."

"Meanwhile, I'll catch up with him," Jane said exultantly. "After this year, I'll be in college."

They didn't seem to care whether Julie joined the conversation or not, but she intervened. "What kind of job do you have?"

"I'm an activities facilitator. Mostly snorkeling and diving. I'm based on Coral Island, showing people the marine life around there and on other parts of the reef. When I do go back to school, I'll take up marine biology, so all this is going to contribute in the long run."

"And where does that leave me?" Jane said. "Since Leslie prefers to be submerged, that may leave me to take care of the family business, and I'm expected to take up agriculture when I go to college."

"What kind of family business do you have?" Julie forced herself to respond.

"Sugar. What else?" Jane laughed. "But personally, I'd rather be a dancer. I had a part with a ballet company from Melbourne when they performed here a couple of years ago. Just a minor part, chorus."

"I should have guessed. That's what Dad came to find out about. Sugar."

"Guess what part Jane played in the ballet?" Leslie said. "A sugar plum fairy, no less. It runs in the family."

The car rounded a corner and Julie saw a sheet of gray-blue water extending before them. "The ocean!" she cried.

"This is the Cairns Esplanade," Mr. Donaldson said. "We came a little out of our way to show it to you. It's rather famous for its birds. I expect you'll see a lot more of it."

"Our hotel is located right across from it," Mr. Blacker said, and Julie hoped they would stop, but they sped on.

"I hope you'll see a lot of the ocean while you're here, too," Leslie added. "I'm planning to submerge you, if it's okay with your dad."

"Julie should definitely see the Great Barrier Reef, and Les is the one to show it to her," Mrs. Donaldson said.

"I'm looking forward to that," Les said in a voice that was too booming and hearty for someone, like Julie, who was still dazed from being hurtled across the world. Out of her time zone and hurting for sleep, she felt almost disembodied. Leslie might not want to show her the reef if he'd stop to discover what a zero she was.

The car pulled up at the Donaldsons' and everyone got out. They lived some distance from the town of Cairns in a house that was set up on supports so high that they could drive their car under it, for it formed a carport. As they drove in, Julie also noticed that the space under the house sheltered a clothes line and provided storage for bikes. A flight of steps led up to the house, which was surrounded by an open veranda. All the houses nearby were similarly constructed.

"Do you have flooding here? Is that why your houses are set up off the ground?" Julie's dad asked.

"Not so much that, as that this is the tropics. The breeze flowing through that space helps cool the house," Mr. Donaldson explained.

"Come out in back, we'll get the fire going." Leslie's hand gripped Julie's bare arm, and she was conscious of a force that was disturbing. She didn't know Leslie well enough for him to be that chummy. He wasn't allowing time to get acquainted.

"Leslie, leave her alone. She said she wanted a shower. She's coming to my room to get organized. Julie, he's planning to monopolize you. He got special leave to come home from his job for the weekend when he heard we'd have an American girl visiting. Watch out. He has designs on you." Jane said it in a teasing voice without malice, and Les made a comical face at his sister.

"She's betraying confidential information," Leslie said, releasing his hold on Julie's arm.

"Come on, you can see my room and change and then we'll listen to music," Jane proposed. "But you don't really need to change if you don't want to. Nobody will be dressed up tonight."

"I just want to get a shower," Julie said, wishing they wouldn't lavish so much attention on her.

She showered and washed her hair, feeling rushed because everyone was waiting for her. The air was muggy in Jane's room, and Jane had put on some music. She rummaged through her suitcase for a presentable pair of shorts. That was what the Donaldsons were wearing. Leslie looked neat and tanned in well-pressed white shorts, and he wore long, white knee socks, which Julie thought must be a strictly Australian style that gave an impression of formality. Jane also wore white shorts and a T-shirt with a picture of a crocodile on it. Julie's shorts were creased from being packed tightly in her suitcase.

"You're all refreshed," Jane said. "Do you want to listen to some records? I have a new tape by Split Enz. Of course, I have a lot of American tapes, too, but I thought

you might like to hear some of our local talent. Cold
Chisel—have you heard that group?" She started to put
some music on her machine, but then she could see out the
window that some kids were piling from a car in front of the
house. "My friends are here. Come on. You can meet
Katherine and the guys."

Jane was full of energy, and she left Julie behind as she
rushed out the door to welcome her friends. Les was waiting outside the door as she followed Jane. "Don't let them
take you over," he said. "You were going to be my partner
tonight. They're not going to deprive me of my first evening with an American beauty."

He had to be kidding! Julie felt anything but beautiful.
Her hair was still damp from the shower, though it was
drying and fluffing out into curls. Her eyes felt irritated
from lack of sleep. "Thanks for trying to make me feel
good," Julie said. "But let's face it, jet lag has made me into
a first-class creep."

Jane and her friends had come in, and they looked at one
another and laughed. "Pardon us for laughing," she said,
"but we've all heard about American slang, and we decided we'd collect some while you were here."

"Creep," Katherine said. "That's a good one."

"Does that sound weird to you?" Julie asked.

Jane and Katherine giggled. "Weird," Jane said. "Let's
write these down and try them on our friends."

"We might start a fad," Katherine agreed. "No offense,
Julie. We just think you have unusual ways of expressing
yourselves."

They walked into the yard where Les was working at a
structure of brick, with a long, metal plate on top, which he
was lubricating with vegetable oil.

"How about you youngsters preparing the onions?" he
asked. Mrs. Donaldson appeared with a platter of lamb

chops and fish filets, meat patties and large sausages. Les arranged them on a large griddle and they started sizzling.

"He gives us the worst job," Jane complained, "but it has to be done." A huge bag of onions sat beside a bowl on a side table, and Jane and Katherine cajoled Richard and John, their boyfriends, to do the chopping while they prepared salads. Mrs. Donaldson placed a tablecloth on a long table and was setting out platters of tropical fruits: papayas, bananas and pineapple.

"You're to help me over here at the barby," Les told Julie, handing her a fork. The two dads were off in a corner having a glass of wine and talking business. Julie turned over a lamb chop and pushed a sausage over to one side of the grill. She felt that people were swirling around her like a kaleidoscope, their voices intermingling in a deafening cacophony. Now and then Leslie said something to her, and she responded without really knowing what she was saying. She had that disembodied spirit feeling again.

The guys had finished a huge bowl of onions, which they dumped onto the griddle along with the meats. Julie half heard the voices of Jane and her friends mixed in with the sizzling food, and when it was done, she consumed her share and settled onto the side of an outdoor lounge beside Les, who became suffocatingly attentive to her. The fire had dwindled down to a bed of softly glowing embers, and the warmth of it made Julie drowsy. She leaned her head against the cushion of the lounge.

"You have such big stars here," she commented. The Donaldsons' house was well away from the lights of the town, and in the blackness thousands of stars were visible, the Milky Way standing out with a clarity Julie had never seen in the densely populated San Francisco peninsula from which she came.

"Just there," Leslie pointed to a kite-shaped group of four stars, "you can see the Southern Cross. I don't believe it's visible in your hemisphere."

"So that's it. Beautiful!" Julie's eyes traveled across the dark sky studded with brilliant stars and she saw one shoot across the sky. She could hear her dad and Mr. Donaldson discussing the problems of the worldwide glut of sugar.

"In the United States," Mr. Blacker was saying, "sugar has bad P.R. There's all this emphasis on being thin and fit. Low-calorie artificial sweeteners are the fad, although some nutritionists are finding problems with them. Sugar, in short, is in bad repute." Her dad's voice faded into a drone. Les was pointing out other features of the heavens, which reeled before her eyes. She vaguely heard one of Jane's friends ask Leslie a question which diverted his attention from Julie, and Julie's head nodded sidewise in the chair, her surroundings blurring into oblivion.

The next thing Julie knew, she was being picked up and carried. Her eyes flew open and she heard a car pulling away and the laughing voices of Julie's friends calling goodbye.

"What happened?" Julie asked. She saw Les's blond head floating above her.

"You fell asleep during my boring lecture about the stars," he said. Julie's father opened the back door of the car and Les started to set her in.

"Oh, I can get in myself," she cried, embarrassed to have ended the party this way. She struggled from his arms to her feet and climbed into the back seat. Les eased himself in beside her.

"It's something of a novelty for the guest of honor to go to sleep at the party," Les said in a good-natured way, which nevertheless made Julie feel uncomfortable. She'd made a fool of herself. She put her hand to her hair. She must look like a scarecrow by now, and Les was not two inches from her, observing her faults.

Les leaned up over the front seat as they started toward the hotel. "Mr. Blacker, I wonder if Julie could come out on the reef next week. See, I'm working out there and I could show her around."

"Julie certainly ought to see the reef," Mr. Blacker said.

"We don't want her to miss any of the sights," Mr. Donaldson said. "Tomorrow, we'll show her some of our rain forests and lakes, and of course, our sugarcane fields."

"Do you skin-dive?" Les turned eagerly to Julie.

"I swim a lot."

"Then I could check you out. That's part of my job. Diving instruction."

"We preferred for Les to go to college this year, but he talked us into letting him keep his job on the reef," Mr. Donaldson said.

"It's all going to be for the better in the long run, father. I'll have a head start when I do get back to school and start taking marine biology."

"If you can ever part with your job," his father remarked sourly.

"What kind of work do you do?"

"You'll see. When can she come out, Mr. Blacker? I'm due back at the island on Monday."

"I won't be able to bring her out until the weekend. I have several meetings and appointments during the next few days."

"Well, then, you should let her come out during the week while you're busy. We'll take good care of her."

"I don't know about Julie going out there alone," Mr. Blacker said.

"Oh, she won't be alone. She'll be with me, and since I'm an activities director out there, I'll see that she won't get bored. We have great accommodations—these nice little cottages in the woods."

Mr. Blacker cleared his throat. "Well, I meant—"

"I think Julie's father may be worrying about a chaperone. Julie is rather young to be going off by herself. You're how old, Julie?"

"Sixteen. I could handle it," Julie said. Les put his arm around her and looked down at her approvingly, making her wonder if she could handle it.

Les continued his persuasion. "Besides, Mr. Blacker, she'll be with other girls there. I'll introduce her to some of the girls who work there, and of course, she'll meet other guests. Alone is what she won't be over at Coral Island."

"We'll see." Julie's father said in a terse voice, which indicated that the conversation was closed.

Julie felt light-headed and disembodied, as if Les and her father were talking about someone else and she didn't need to enter the conversation herself. Les was unreal. She'd only known him for a few hours; she looked like a geek and he was ready to take her to this island. What was he up to? She was too tired to figure it out. It was a relief to turn the corner and see the trees silhouetted against the ocean, which gleamed like an unruffled sheet of silver in the moonlight. Along the Esplanade, hills arose around a protected bay, and the water ebbed and rose soundlessly, with no surf or breakers, leaving a mud flat along the seawall.

"We'll see you tomorrow morning," Les said.

"Don't come out early," Julie instructed, trying not to yawn.

Les gave her shoulder an affectionate squeeze. "Sleepyhead!" he teased. "You'd better get plenty of rest tonight if you're going to hang around with me. We Aussies like to keep moving."

Julie didn't want to hear about action. All she wanted was sleep, and Leslie's vigorous hospitality only made her more tired. His accent, however intriguing, only reminded her that he was a foreigner she hadn't known very long. If her dad and his hadn't been with them, in fact, Julie might have been a little scared of Les, who had come on to her very strong from the first.

"Oh, Dad," she said as the taillights of the Donaldsons' car disappeared down the street and they went into their hotel. "I'm so tired I can't think straight."

"I know, honey. It's not easy to come off a flight halfway around the world right into an evening of socializing with strangers—especially when they're as energetic as that Donaldson boy. But now we're back where you can get some rest."

Julie and her dad had single rooms connected by a bath. The evening was muggy, even though it was winter in Australia, and Julie was glad to see a rotating fan on the ceiling of her room. She wanted to talk to someone about Les and his suffocating attention to her, but there was no one to confide in. She didn't think her dad would want to be bothered with such a discussion. He had more important things on his mind, even though he had already figured out that Les was a supercharged guy.

"I'm just going to hit the sack, Dad," she said.

"Me too," Mr. Blacker said, yawning. "See you in the morning, honey. They have a breakfast bar downstairs."

Julie lost no time in falling into a deep sleep, and when she awoke, the morning was half gone. Opening the door into her dad's room, she found him gone. Had they left for the cane fields without her? Julie felt panicky. What would she do all day alone? She quickly ran back into her room and dressed in a pair of shorts, a T-shirt, and her jogging shoes.

Downstairs, she looked for her dad in the breakfast bar, but there was no sign of him. Anyway, she needed something to eat, and she scanned the menu. Weird! They offered spaghetti on toast, baked beans on toast or creamed corn on toast. Even though the Australians were basically like Americans, they did have their different tastes. Julie chose a glass of orange juice, some raisin toast and a dish of papaya, and sat down under an umbrella on the hot patio.

Since her dad still hadn't put in an appearance when she'd finished, she wandered across the street to the Esplanade, a grassy strip of lawn that extended far down the edge of the ocean. She could hear the soft sound of a dove, and overhead she saw a tree filled with bright red and green birds like small parrots. The tide was low, leaving mud flats dotted with ponds and threaded with rivulets. Hundreds of birds stalked over the mud: slender egrets, stately ibis and a variety of sandpipers, all extracting food from the rich silt. White terns skimmed low over the scene, hovering and plucking snails from the surface. Julie sat on a bench to watch a skein of huge black and white pelicans soar in graceful formation through the air. She felt a hand on her shoulder.

"There you are! Your dad thought you ought to be allowed to sleep, so I offered to wait here. I've been walking up and down, watching the birds. The others went out to the house. I'm supposed to bring you on whenever you're ready. Have you had breakfast? You look great! You seem to be caught up on your sleep."

Les looked even more enchanting than he had the night before. "I was worried when I couldn't find Dad," she said. "But you're right. I did get caught up on my sleep."

The sunlight filtering through the palms gilded his hair and made his brows golden against his tanned skin. His eyes smiled from beneath sun-bleached lashes. He didn't seem the foreign stranger he had been last night, but a familiar figure, the only person she knew in this faraway land.

"I'm ready," she said.

Chapter Three

As the car sped through Cairns and into the outskirts, it passed through vast fields of sugarcane. A few miles out, Les explained that they were passing the Donaldsons' fields. The cane stretched on and on, broken occasionally by a field of stubble where the plants had recently been harvested. "We let it grow for two years, and then cut it," he explained.

"Dad would like for me to be a cane farmer and take over the business, but I've got the sea in my blood. I hope your father will let you go to the reef tomorrow and I'll show you why I'm fascinated. You'll see things you never dreamed could exist. Surprises, wonders, mysteries..."

"You must have discovered a sunken treasure," Julie said teasingly.

"Wait and see." Leslie's eyes gleamed with anticipation.

"I wonder if Dad will really let me go. At home my parents are so picky about what I do. If Dad isn't going, he'll probably think I shouldn't go there alone."

"Alone? You'll be with me."

"He'll think that's worse."

"Don't you lot do as you please in America? The land of the free, isn't it?"

"Not until you're eighteen," Julie corrected. "Until then, we're very much oppressed."

"Your father has to let you come. Otherwise, I won't get to see you anymore. If you're a visitor on the island, I'll be able to show you the ropes. You can be in my diving group. I'll put it up to your dad on an educational basis. He'll be signing you up for a class, and I'll be responsible for you."

Julie looked at Les, his hair shining in the slanting rays of the sun that came through the side window of the car. His profile was just about perfect. His tanned, athletic hands rested skillfully on the steering wheel. At home, he'd be classified as a hunk. Over in Blossom Valley, Julie wouldn't have had a chance with such a guy as Les. Everybody would be chasing him. A girl like Chrissie Quaill might even abandon her boyfriend, Adam, if someone like Les Donaldson should stroll by. Even a popular girl like Marcie McCord would flip over him. Mike Washburn would be left in the shade by the vibrant Les. And here he was urging her to go out on this fabulous reef with him. Surely he hadn't taken a good look at her—or maybe he was under orders from his dad to give her a whirl—anyway, Les Donaldson was definitely in the dreamboat category, and Julie felt it was an unreal scene for her to be in his company.

Jane was waiting at the door when the car pulled up at the elevated Donaldson house. "Les," she complained. "You've been monopolizing Julie again. I've been waiting all morning to talk to her."

"Honest, Jane, I brought her over as soon as she woke up."

"It's true. I slept in. I was really bushed."

"Bushed. That's a new one. I'll write that down. Come on, let's play those records we didn't get to play last night."

Julie said that the Split Enz and the Cold Chisel groups sounded similar to American rock bands. "What about country and western? We play a lot of that in California."

"We have our own Australian country music—from the bush ballads," Jane said, riffling through her albums. "Here's our most famous singer, Slim Dusty. He probably doesn't sound like your American western."

"Right. He has his own Australian quality," Julie agreed after she had heard the singer. "You have a neat record collection."

"Neat." Jane grinned and jotted the word down in her notebook. "All our friends are envious because we're entertaining an American," she said. "At school, they'll be asking me about it, and I'll tell them about your American expressions."

So that was it, Julie reflected. She was a curiosity to be shown and talked about to the Donaldsons' Australian friends. That explained Les's interest in her. But it was fair enough. If kids from overseas visited Blossom Valley, she'd be showing them off, too. They'd be like the exotic foreign exchange students at school, from places like Finland and Argentina, and everyone was curious about them.

"Maybe I'd better start a list of weird Australian expressions," Julie said. "Your name over in our country would be pronounced Jane, and not Jine."

"I'll be careful to use the King's English," Jane said, laughing. She had dark hair, like her father. She was as attractive as Les, in her own way. They were both carefree, happy young people, open and uncomplicated.

When she and Jane joined their parents, Julie saw that Les had her father engaged in earnest conversation. He was acting very dignified and mature. Julie felt her skin suffuse with a glow of embarrassment. He was arguing that Julie would be safe with him on Coral Island.

"All the equipment is furnished," she heard him say, "snorkels, fins, an Aqualung if she reaches that stage. Mr. Blacker, it would be a crime for Julie to be in this part of Australia without seeing the coral gardens and the reef creatures. She can't leave here without doing some diving. It will be a real education for her. Every evening we show movies—history of the reef, identification and behavior of the fish, types of coral. She can't miss it."

Her father looked wary of Les. Too bad that he was so good-looking. That was probably what was arousing doubts that he could trust Julie on Coral Island. Mr. Blacker was paying very close attention to Les, sizing him up. One way or another, her dad was going to regret bringing her along on the trip to Australia. Either she'd stay with him, getting in his way while he was trying to gather material for his articles, or she'd be off on her own, and he'd be so worried about what she was doing that he wouldn't be able to concentrate on his news gathering.

Julie remembered all the arguments in the family when she had started going out with Mike. They thought he was too old for her. She'd only been fourteen and Mike sixteen. When he finally gave in her dad made the condition that she couldn't ride in a car which Mike was driving. They had to be chauffeured around by her parents. She had to give Mike credit for going along with that. It had proved he really loved her, when he could endure having her parents around all the time. Later, when Harlan learned to drive and they let him take the car, they also had to allow Mike to drive Julie, although they had never gotten over being nervous about it. No wonder Mike had found other interests than overprotected Julie when he went off to college.

With all the rules and regulations she had grown up with, it would be a miracle if her father allowed her to go to the island with Les. There were just her dad and herself. She felt sorry for him, being burdened with an important assignment and under pressure from one of the world's most spectacular guys, who wished to spirit his daughter off to a tropical island, not just for the evening, but for the rest of the week. She could see her dad's eyes darting this way and that, moving from herself to Les, and then dropping speculatively to some papers he'd been working on with Les's father. She could imagine what was going through his mind, and it gave her a tingle of excitement, as well as arousing sympathy for her dad. She wasn't sure he was equipped to handle such a decision. If she could only get him off by himself and talk to him! Les was leaning tensely toward him, persuading, his gray eyes compelling her dad to consent.

"What is Les cooking up?" Jane asked, her eyes following Julie's to her brother's earnest entreaty to Mr. Blacker. "Aha! He's inviting you out to his island! 'Come into my parlor, said the spider to the fly.'"

At Julie's startled expression, Jane laughed. "I'm only teasing, Les is as harmless as a koala. But it isn't fair! He's scheming to take you to Coral Island, and I won't get to see you anymore."

"Can't you go to the island too?" Julie asked.

Jane squeezed her face into a grimace. "I have to be in school."

"So you can't entertain her, anyway," he retorted.

Julie's father had a perplexed expression on his face. He didn't seem to know what to say.

"We were going to show the Blackers some of the countryside," Mr. Donaldson intervened. "Perhaps we could sort it out on the way."

Julie's father seemed relieved to have the pressure off momentarily.

"I hope we'll see a kangaroo," Julie said, "and a koala."

The Donaldsons looked at one another warily. "We might run across an agile wallaby," Mr. Donaldson said.

"I've never seen a koala outside of a zoo," Jane added.

"In Brisbane, there's a koala park where lots of them live, but up here, no chance," Leslie said.

"I thought I'd see kangaroos hopping everywhere," Julie said.

"Not anymore. I suppose they once were plentiful, but the wild territory where they used to roam has been farmed, and they've been driven back into the bush."

Dry cane fields rose on either side of the road as far as one could see. "Look!" Julie exclaimed. "There's smoke ahead. It's a fire!"

"Burning off a cane field," Mr. Donaldson explained. Fire licked along the edge of the road and was advancing into the field. "You see, it's been set in several places along the road."

Beyond the field, the car stopped for a narrow-gauge train pulling rickety wire cages on wheels. The cages were filled with foot-long sections of cane, which Mr. Donaldson explained were being taken to a sugar mill to be ground up. "We'll visit the mill tomorrow." Mr. Donaldson addressed the last remark to Julie's father.

"You won't be going there, I hope," Leslie whispered to Julie. "You would be bored at the sugar mill, when you could be diving in the coral gardens with me." Leslie's breath stirred the hair around Julie's ears and disturbed her. Squeezed into the backseat, she was thrown against him whenever the car hit a bump, which was often. The road had become rough after they left the vicinity of the town. Where there were not potholes, it was unpaved.

Jolting against him, she became superconscious of him and a fear of going to the island with him possessed her. Even with her dad and his parents sitting right in the front seat, she was uncomfortable with his insistence. Could she handle being alone with such a guy?

"Look back," Jane said. "You'll see one of the landmarks of Cairns." A perfect pyramid-shaped mountain dominated the landscape. "I wish you had come in October," she continued. "That's when we have the Fun in the Sun festival in Cairns. The town is all done up with flowers, everyone dresses in south seas style, and we have jazz concerts, parades, dances, sometimes a circus. You should have seen Leslie at the last one. He was in the crocodile race."

"Don't let her give you the impression that I was competing with a crocodile," Leslie said. "To be accurate, she should have said that I was a crocodile jockey. Some of the business leaders of the town sponsor crocs, and Father let me be the jockey of his—that is, I was to prod our reptile toward the finish line."

"How gross!" Julie exclaimed. "Weren't you afraid the crocodile would bite you?"

"The crocs are muzzled. Their jaws are tied shut with ribbons. We weren't allowed to touch the beasts. We could only shout, stamp and clap our hands together. That's not all that goes on at the festival. The abos have a corroboree with their ancient weapons—spears, shields and boomerangs."

"Abos?" Julie questioned.

"The aborigines. They were the inhabitants of Australia before the European explorers came here. They were fierce hunters. Of course, a lot of them live around Cairns still, but they don't practice their ancient customs. They live pretty much like the rest of us."

Jane and Julie conversed then, and Leslie looked out the window, deep in thought.

"The other night when I met your friends, John and Richard," Julie said, "I was sort of out of it. I'd been sitting up all night and it didn't register on me which one was your boyfriend and which was Katherine's."

Jane's face illuminated at the mention of their names. "Richard, of course," she answered.

"Are they in your class at school?" Julie asked.

"No. Katherine and I go to a girls' school and they go to a boys' school. But John and Richard play soccer with Katherine's brother. That's how we met them."

"Do you go to their soccer games?"

"We never miss."

Leslie ceased his staring out the window and hung over the front seat where he could get the attention of Julie's father, and he resumed his harangue to get Julie to spend a few days on the reef. Julie could tell by the set of her father's jaw that he felt himself pushed to the wall. At home, he might have said, "We'll see what Julie's mother says about it."

As for Julie, she had those weird mixed feelings. On one hand, going out on the reef was probably the most exciting thing she'd ever had a chance to do. She would practically die if her dad said no. But on the other hand, did she want to go with Leslie? He was not only too attractive, but too foreign. He had this soft, ingratiating accent, his sentences ending on an interrogative tone, as though he were constantly seeking approval. That kind of voice was disarming. It would take her dad off guard and force him to let Julie go. She might find herself on the island with Leslie and unable to resist his charm—and what might happen then? Either that or he would find her a dud and dump her as

Mike had, and there she would be, sitting alone out on a speck in the Pacific Ocean. He was probably a champion swimmer, and he might not find her diving up to his standards. And weren't there venomous sea snakes, dangerous octopi, or those great flapping rays one saw on the TV nature programs? Couldn't a giant clam snap her foot off?

Mr. Donaldson stopped the car on a side road. "I thought you'd like a look at the mangroves," he said, "and then we'll go on to show you the rain forest."

Leslie stayed close behind Julie as the party picked its way through the tangle of prop roots that angled strangely out from the trunks of the mangroves. Mr. Donaldson was explaining that there were twenty-eight different kinds of mangroves in this forest, and that the knobby things that Julie was tripping over were pneumatophores, aerial roots by which the trees breathed. That made Julie feel they were part human, and she tried not to step on the protruding knobs.

"I think your father is caving in," Leslie's voice was again disturbingly close to Julie's ear. They had come to a slough. Reflections of the mangroves in the dark pool shattered as a brilliant azure kingfisher darted from a partly submerged branch at the edge of the water. It was cool and shady. Julie looked down and saw herself and Leslie mirrored in the pool. A leaf fell onto the surface and distorted their images.

"It's so peaceful here in the forest," Julie said.

"Even more so down in the coral gardens under the sea," Leslie said, his words conveying confidence that she would go with him to the reef. Why was he so eager for her to go? There must be other girls there.

They proceeded away from the mangroves, past banana plantations; the heavy stalks of fruit protected by blue and silver plastic bags.

"That's to speed their ripening and also to repel the flying foxes," Mr. Donaldson explained.

"Flying foxes!" Julie exclaimed. "Will we see one?"

"They're all asleep now. They fly at night, but we may see some sleeping in the trees. We call them flying foxes, but what they really are is bats. Fruit bats. They can wreak havoc on the banana and papaya crops."

Presently they stopped at a tree where some of the creatures could be seen hanging upside down from the boughs of a tree.

"You'll find the fish around the reef are much prettier than these bats," Leslie said. He was not going to let the subject drop. To Mr. Blacker, he added, "Julie will see parrot fish, grouper, bass, and barramundi very closely down there. She'll get a first-hand view of the plants and animals interacting with one another. It will be a real lesson in ecology."

"I wish I could skip school and go along," Jane said. Julie wished so, too. If Jane came along, Leslie would be pretty innocuous, but alone, he might lose the inhibitions he had around his family, and he might cause problems for her.

The car had arrived at another turnoff, and the Donaldsons got out a picnic basket to take into the rain forest. They entered a jungle of giant trees whose trunks were embellished with ferns and orchids. Birds called and twittered in the canopy, and as the party walked along the trail, they often had to climb over or under fallen tree trunks. Julie felt a sharp pain in the calf of her leg and saw that a trailing palm frond had cut into her flesh.

"That's what we call the 'Wait a Bit,'" Mrs. Donaldson said, extricating the growth from Julie's leg. Julie saw the cruel barbs along the length of it. Mrs. Donaldson found Julie a Band-Aid in her purse.

"You won't find any of those obnoxious things under the sea," Les told her.

"You have a one-track mind," Julie said, laughing. His persistence was becoming comical.

"I just don't want you to miss out on the Great Barrier Reef," he said. They all sat down and spread out a picnic beside a tree around whose trunk writhed heavy vine branches. A colorful bird with a bright red patch around its eye, a gold breast, and brilliant green wings flashed onto a branch above them. "The fig bird," Mr. Donaldson said. "He'll plant a fig seed in the top of a big tree and the fig will sprout, sending roots down the trunk toward the ground. Eventually the fig will strangle and kill the tree, and the fig foliage will take over in the canopy, just as it has here. This is a classic strangler fig."

Julie looked up at the awesome vine, and Leslie began his petition to Julie's father once more.

"Mr. Blacker," he urged, "if Julie were going out to the reef tomorrow, she'd have to leave on the 8:30 boat. We'll have to call over there as soon as we get back and make sure there's a room for her. I won't be able to take her to dinner, because I have to eat with the staff people, but I can see that she's seated with some congenial people. I'll be showing movies in the evening which she can attend, and of course, I'll be able to teach her to skin dive along with other visitors on the island. That's the main part of my job. She'll come out with a new skill."

"It isn't fair," Jane complained. "I'm going to miss out."

All the Donaldsons had their eyes fixed on Julie's father. He seemed to be cornered as he leaned back against the fig vine nursing a cold drink can. If he said no, the Donaldsons would think he didn't trust Les.

"How about it, Julie? Is this something you want to do?"

"Of course, Dad," Julie blurted, glancing toward Leslie, over whose face a satisfied smile was spreading.

"Well, then." Mr. Blacker looked at Les's parents. "We'll make the arrangements as soon as we get back."

Chapter Four

Les, who knew the schedules of the catamarans that went to the reef, was the one who telephoned for the reservations, both on the boat and at the hotel on Coral Island. He looked worried as he phoned. "There aren't many rooms available," he said. "It's a small island and they don't like a crowd there." But as he talked to the people at the hotel, whom he seemed to know well, his face smoothed into a smile.

"We're in luck," he said. "There was a cancellation, and it's yours."

After Les had made arrangements to take Julie to the boat the next morning, Julie began to have qualms about going to the island with Les. She didn't know him that well. She'd only been in his company along with his family and her dad. He might be a totally different person when she was alone with him on that island. What was her dad thinking of to let her go? Did he just want to get rid of her so he could do his work? Did he just suddenly not care what became of her? Now that she'd been rejected by Mike Washburn, why not by her dad as well?

Back home, they'd never have let her go, for instance, up to Lake Tahoe for even a weekend with a guy—or anyplace else, for that matter. They wouldn't even let her stay out until after midnight. So what had happened? Why had her dad changed his attitude so radically? Julie felt as if she were being put adrift in a boat with no oars, and that she could be swallowed up in this unexpected adventure.

The fan revolved around and around, casting an unsettling shadow on the ceiling of her room, reminding her that she was far away from her friends, her mother and Harlan, from everything familiar—except, of course, her dad. She could hear him brushing his teeth behind the door of the bathroom that connected their rooms. She knocked hesitantly. "Dad?"

"I'm almost finished, honey; just a jiff." He turned off the water and opened the door. "It's all yours," he said.

"I didn't want in," she explained. She wasn't accustomed to talking over her feelings with her dad. A lot of the time, she just kept them to herself because it was embarrassing to discuss really personal things. If it was something that wasn't too painful to talk about, it was her mother she went to. Once in a while, if she could catch him, she'd talk over some problems with Harlan. He could be a pretty good listener and give some advice on problems connected with school or grades. Really personal concerns, like about guys, she either kept to herself or talked over with her best friend, Kim.

Now there was nobody except her dad. He probably shouldn't be bothered with such a discussion, but he was involved in this. It was practically his fault that she was going to be stuck on an island with a handsome hunk she hadn't even known before yesterday.

"Dad," she said, for he was waiting quizzically to hear what she had to say. She rushed on: "Do you really think it's okay for me to go to that island? Because if you don't, it's all right. I won't go. I'll tell him tomorrow morning I decided not to."

"Don't you want to go, Julie? I thought you were eager to go. I want you to have a good time on our trip."

"But I never—back home, you wouldn't—Mom might not like for me to be out there—not only after twelve o'clock, but for a whole week."

Mr. Blacker walked over and sat in the cramped chair in front of the dresser with his back to Julie. He looked at her in the mirror.

"I thought about that, baby, and I made the decision to let you go because I thought you'd enjoy yourself with the young people on that island more than you would hanging around with me at the sugar conference. Of course," he turned and looked at her directly instead of at her reflection in the mirror and then gave her the one-sided, comical grin he had used since she was a little kid to let her know that all was right with the world, "I would have enjoyed showing off my beautiful daughter to those stodgy old sugar barons. I know you like swimming, and you're going to see marvelous things on that reef. I thought about how I would have liked to see that when I was your age. In fact, I'd still like to see it. I was thinking I'd come out on the weekend and you could show me around."

"That would be terrific, Dad, but do you think it's suitable for me—you know, to be staying by myself when Les— I don't know him all that well, what kind of a guy he is." There, it was out. Julie hadn't believed she could bring up the subject of a guy with her dad.

Mr. Blacker smiled and leaned closer to Julie. "Do *you* think it's suitable? A young lady who can make a trip halfway around the world ought to be responsible enough to take a short side trip out to a fabulous island on the world's greatest coral reef."

"But I came over here with you, and now—"

"Julie, honey." Her father leaned more earnestly toward her. "What your mother and I hoped all through the years we've been raising you is that our family values would get permanently programmed into you, so that when you found yourself on your own you'd have built in guidelines that would give you confidence in your own behavior—following your own sense of right. Have we succeeded in building a basis for you to make your own decisions when we're not around?"

"Then do you and Mom consider me—kind of finished already?"

"Well, Julie, you're not a little kid anymore. Suppose we look at this trip to the island as a kind of test of your ability to handle a little independence?"

"Suppose I flunk that test, Dad?"

"If I had any inkling that you would, I wouldn't have consented to let you go."

"You trust me a lot, Dad." Julie said it with a touch of incredulity.

"Why shouldn't I? Haven't I known you for sixteen years?"

"Sure. But it's not me I'm worried about. It's Les, and we've only known him for a day."

"They seem to be a nice family, the Donaldsons. Pretty close."

"Yeah, they get along well together."

"I'm betting that Leslie has approximately the same kind of standards you have, Julie."

"But he's a guy. And he's an Australian. We don't know much about how they operate, or what's okay for them."

"We're all members of the human race, Julie. He's probably not much different from your brother, Harlan—or your old boyfriend—what was his name? If you'll just behave as you would around them, then you'll have my blessing to enjoy the reef without a lot of groundless fears and apprehensions. It's going to be a great adventure for you, Julie. Let's get to bed so you'll be rested for your trip."

"Thanks, Dad." Julie went over and planted a kiss on his cheek, and as she did she noticed how much gray hair her dad had developed on the sides of his head, and how wrinkles were coming around his eyes. He probably wanted her to get responsible so he wouldn't have to make her decisions for her anymore. As he went into his own room, she noticed that her dad's shoulders were sloping a little more than they used to do. She looked at herself in the mirror, and saw somebody who was practically an adult. No wonder her dad thought she was mature enough to go out on her own. What about him? Was he going to be lonely this week, in a hotel room by himself?

That thought returned to her the next morning when she locked her suitcase for the trip on the boat. Her dad came downstairs with her and they found Les pacing back and forth on the sidewalk in front of the hotel. Across the street on the Esplanade hundreds of lorikeets screeched and scolded in the big trees, and a few stately ibis pranced about looking for crumbs left by picnickers.

"I was afraid you'd change your mind, that you weren't coming," Leslie said. Julie saw the tense set of his face smooth into relief.

"Of course not. I have a reservation, don't I?" she said, her smile a little strained, for basically, Leslie was still a stranger.

"I'll get that, sir," Leslie said, snatching Julie's suitcase from her dad. Julie thought that his calling her father "sir" was a good sign. It showed respect, as if he wasn't the sort to overstep any bounds, and yet, the very fact that he had her suitcase with her most intimate possessions in it, made her uneasy. His hair shone in the sunlight that filtered through the trees as they walked along the Esplanade. A string of pelicans soared low over the bay toward the pier, drawing Julie's eyes toward the assortment of ships, yachts and boats anchored there.

"Can we see our ship from here?" she asked.

"It's on the other side," Les explained. It's called *The Dolphin.* Les was wearing a T-shirt with a picture of a catamaran rising on a wave, and below it was written "Coral Island." He wore a crisply pressed pair of white Bermuda shorts, white shoes and white knee socks.

"I'll be on duty, so I won't be able to stay with you, Julie. I'm supposed to mingle with the passengers and give announcements."

"I'll be okay. Don't worry about me," Julie said. She moved her hand over by her dad's, and he squeezed it, giving her a reassuring smile.

They passed from the Esplanade onto the pier. People were buying tickets to various excursions around the reef. Sails were being rigged, and a fishing boat had set out into the bay, a cloud of silver gulls swirling about it.

"I was really surprised to hear there was a hotel on the Great Barrier Reef," Julie said to Les as they walked down the pier toward *The Dolphin*'s berth. "I always thought it was just a big pile of rocks protruding from the sea where you would find all these fabulous shells."

Leslie laughed. "Most of the reef is covered with water," he said. "You won't find it protruding, except for a scattering of islands and cays. Maybe you don't realize that the reef is 1,200 miles long. It stretches from New Guinea almost to Brisbane, halfway down the Australian coast. It would be halfway down the west coast of the United States—perhaps as long as the coast of California."

"I had a totally wrong impression," Julie said. They had reached *The Dolphin*, around which a large collection of people had assembled. Julie noted families with small children, a group of older people with name tags and some kids about her age wearing backpacks.

"A lot of these are day people," Les explained. "They'll go out and spend a few hours on the island and then come back on the three o'clock run. Actually, what we call a hotel is really a group of cabins, and a very limited number of people can stay overnight on the island. That was why we were so lucky to get that cancellation for you."

"I'd better check to see if I can get in next weekend," Mr. Blacker said. "I'll come out and have a look at the island and come home with Julie."

"It's usually booked," Les said, "but being on the staff, maybe I can pull some strings and get you in. You'll be in those sugar industry meetings all this week, sir?"

"Yes, and I'll be ready for a rest by the weekend."

"I'll be an old hand on the island by then, Dad. I can be your guide."

"I'll see that she's a good one," Leslie said, viewing Julie with what she was afraid was too much enthusiasm.

Did her dad notice? He didn't seem to. "They're about to push off, honey. You better get aboard." He gave Julie a little farewell hug. "Have a great time."

"I'll phone you, Daddy," Julie said, feeling bereft to leave him. She had never been shoved out on her own before, much less in a foreign country.

On the ship, Leslie said, "You can sit either upstairs or down, or just roam around. There's a refreshment bar downstairs. Here, I'll get you an orange squash for the road."

The passengers were streaming into the craft, most of them choosing seats outside of the aft deck. Julie decided to stay at the back rail so she could watch the shore receding and wave to her dad until he became a little speck in the distance and she could see him leaving the pier. Someone had called Leslie to come to the front of the ship, for the ship belonged to the island, and Les was now on duty.

She was surprised to hear his young voice coming over the loudspeaker. He was giving the passengers a description of the reef they would soon see. "The Great Barrier Reef is not a single reef," he began, "but a chain of hundreds of small reefs covering about 80,000 square miles." He continued, describing the origin of the reef some two million years ago as three hundred and forty species of coral extended their polyps searching for food and built up limestone skeletons beneath them. Algae cemented the limestone together, creating a cement-like substance. This great chain of reefs, he explained, created a barrier between the northeast coast of Australia and the Coral Sea, with a fifty-mile lagoon between, where one of the most diverse collections of marine life in the world flourishes.

"As for Coral Island," he went on, "the ocean through the years deposited so much crushed coral, shells and algae that a permanent cay came into being. Beach rock formed and fresh water accumulated under the ground. Seabirds landed, some of them bringing seeds on their feet or feathers. Forests sprouted from these seeds, and as you wander about the tracks through the forests, we'll explain more about life on Coral Island."

Next the ship's hostess came on the loudspeaker and described the eating facilities on the island, which consisted of a restaurant for those who were staying over, and a snack bar for the day visitors.

Julie saw various passengers approaching Les to ask him questions. He was going to be pestered constantly, and might not have much time for her.

Coral Island came into view on the horizon as a tiny green mound, growing larger as they approached. Les shook off his questioners and advanced toward Julie, his eyes squinting from beneath his sunbleached brows, his face glowing from the combined radiance of sunlight and sea.

"We'll be docking in about seven minutes," he told her. "Just there," he pointed to a structure which emerged from the trees as they approached, "that's the lodge, and the cabins where you'll stay are hidden by the foliage. We lot— the staff, stay back in the bunkhouses in the middle of the island."

"It's beautiful. Coral Island. It sounds like a jewel."

"Yes, it's a little gem set in silver sand."

"I was impressed with the knowledge of the reef you showed in your announcement. You have a great speaking voice."

"I'm glad you think so, Julie. There's nothing I'd rather do than impress you. Of course, I've made that speech dozens of times. I feel I should know more about the reef. Some day, when I'm a marine biologist, I'll tell you the rest."

The Dolphin was easing into the pier. "I have to go on duty now," Les said, with a little frown. "I have to help with the luggage." He left Julie alone at the rail to make her way up the ramp to the long pier. She saw Les loading suitcases onto a motorized carrier. When the vehicle was full, Les jogged down the pier to catch up with her, and grabbed her arm.

"They keep you busy," Julie observed. "Listen, if you have jobs to do, don't worry about me. I can sit on the beach, or whatever." She breathed in the zesty, briny air of the island.

"I didn't invite you over here to spend time by yourself. A lot of my time can include you. I have to take groups on nature walks and organize the snorkelers—that sort of thing. You'll be part of it."

"Don't let me interfere with your work." The pair stopped beside the luggage cart and Julie pointed out her suitcase, which Les extricated from the rest.

"I'll take you to register." He led Julie to a building where she signed in. She could smell a heady, tropical perfume from a flowering tree. They found her cabin, Number 5. It was set under a canopy of tall trees, and as they ascended the steps to the rustic building, Julie thrilled to see a large white heron flap from the roof. Les turned the key in the lock, coming in behind her to set the suitcase on the floor of a comfortable room with a ceiling fan which seemed to be standard equipment in Australia.

"Do you like it?" Les asked.

Julie pulled the curtains and looked out the window into a forest of lacy palms and other vegetation. "I even have a porch," she said, opening the door and stepping out onto the veranda, where there was a small table and a couple of chairs. "This would be a good place to read."

"I doubt if I'm going to leave you enough time to do much reading." Les stepped out on the porch and stood close beside her, looking down into her eyes. A little shiver made prickles on her arm where it touched his.

A couple of girls wearing Coral Island T-shirts like Les's walked along the path beside Julie's cabin.

"Hi, Les," one of them called.

"Are you coming to check in?" the other asked. "We'll wait for you." They looked curiously at Julie.

"In a minute," he said, frowning. The girls walked on, one of them glancing back and tittering.

"They're on the housekeeping staff," Les explained. "Since I had the weekend off, I have to report for duty and find out what my schedule is for the rest of the week. What a nuisance! I wish I could spend all my time with you. Maybe I'll ask for a few more days off."

"I don't want you to go to any trouble because of me," Julie insisted. "I'll be fine. You go on about your business. I'm going to unpack and go down to that gorgeous beach to catch some rays."

"What an expression! I'll remember to tell Jane. She can add it to her list of Americanisms. After I check in, I'll sneak back and join you on the beach." He gave Julie a casual hug, and then he sprinted down the path over which the two girls had passed.

Chapter Five

Julie watched Les disappear where the path led into dense vegetation. Les was a very active, physical guy. Even though he was attractive, she felt a twinge of regret that she was on this island with him, all by herself. He was sending out signals that he really liked her. What would she do if he came on too strong? At home, it was simple to put a guy off. All you had to do was say, "I have to run, my friend Kim is waiting for me," or if you wanted to turn down a date, just say you had previous plans. There were loads of excuses: homework, you had to help your mom clean house, you'd promised to baby-sit, and so forth. Out here, she was at Les's disposal for the rest of the week. Could she handle it? Was she worrying needlessly? Like her dad said, anyone who came halfway around the world ought to be able to take care of herself. But Les had already started hugging. Things could get out of hand for someone as inexperienced as Julie.

Maybe, however, he was a chronic hugger and that didn't mean anything to him, so Julie decided to forget it. She looked through her suitcase, the contents of which were depressingly unsuitable for Coral Island. Julie had seen some girls in cute cover-ups going to the beach. Her wardrobe didn't include anything like that. Julie's bathing suit was the same one she'd used for her high-school swimming class. Conservative and functional. The girls going past her cabin were wearing very decorative, minimal suits. She just wasn't equipped for Coral Island. It was a drag to be going to the beach alone, anyway. She stopped by the snack stand, bought a cold soda and proceeded over to the beach, which was shaded by slanting coconut palms. She settled herself on her towel and lay down in the sand, inhaling the briny aroma of the sea. She fumbled in her bag for sunglasses. The pure white coral sand was blinding.

"It's a shame to cover up those eyes with shades," someone to the left of her said. The word "shame" came out as "shime" and "shades" as "shides." Julie swiveled her head and saw a guy reclining on a towel a few feet from her. His elbow crooked in the sand so that his arm supported a grinning, ruddy face with a peeling nose. His hair was burnished copper and so were his thick, straight eyebrows.

"I can't stand the glare from the sand," Julie explained.

The guy quit reclining and sat up straight. "You're from America. Your accent gives it away."

"You're the one with the accent," she said. They both laughed.

"Did you come over on the cat this morning?" he asked. To Julie's affirmative nod, he asked, "How did I miss you?"

"I was on the inside, up by the skipper at the last," she said, "so I could hear the announcements more clearly."

"Did you come alone?"

"Sort of," she admitted reluctantly, not wanting to encourage a stranger.

"You came all the way to Australia from America alone!" he exclaimed.

"Not really. I just came alone here to Coral Island. My father came with me from America."

"I'll keep you company when you go back this afternoon. I'm Chris Cavanaugh, from Melbourne."

"You're a long way from home, too," she observed, liking his grin. "But I'm not going back today. I'm staying over all week."

"All week! Why didn't I think of that? I'll tell you why. I can't afford it. I'm backpacking up the coast. Staying at a youth hostel on the Esplanade. Escaping the cold weather in the south."

"I almost forget it's winter in Australia."

"We don't call it winter," Chris explained. "It's called the dry season. I'm about to walk around the island. Care to come?"

"Why not?" The island was so small there would be no harm in walking around it with this brand new acquaintance. Julie liked his breezy style. She folded her towel and stood up. Chris leaped to his feet. He was a couple of inches taller than she was.

"Which way shall we go?" he asked.

"The pier will block our way in that direction. Anyway, I think there's a trail you follow." Julie turned toward the path that ran along the beach and then meandered into the forest. Chris swung into an easy stride beside her, and told her he was taking a jaunt around Australia while trying to decide what to do with his life: he was finished with his secondary education. What kind of school should he attend next? Or should he get some practical experience? "I guess

I'm taking a vacation from the pressure of deciding," he said.

"I'll be faced with that decision next year," she said. "Only my parents will expect me to go to college, and my fate will probably be decided by what college will take me." Julie described the tests she had to take and the competition in the United States to get into the top colleges. She and Chris passed under feathery, gray-green casuarina trees as they turned from the beach toward the interior of the island, which was heavily forested. A spur leading off the path was marked by a sign reading, "Staff only," and a long, barrackslike building was visible among the trees.

"Here's something astonishing!" Chris drew Julie's attention from the staff barracks. He was leaning over a giant spider web woven between two tree trunks.

"Wow!" Julie exclaimed. The spider in the center of the orb had a black and gold body an inch and a half long. Its back legs, which had gold joints, were three inches long. "Astonishing is right!"

They were so intent upon examining the unusual spider that Julie jumped in surprise when she heard Les's voice behind her. "Julie! Is that you?"

Julie whirled around to find Les's questioning eyes moving from her to Chris and back again. "I thought you were going to lie out on the beach," he said. "I was coming over to find you in a few minutes. I had to check the snorkels, masks and flippers we'll be using this afternoon, and I looked over and saw you passing."

"I was on the beach," Julie said. "And Chris here—this is Chris Cavanaugh—Chris, Les Donaldson—was walking around the island, so I came along."

"I was planning to take you around later, when we have the daily nature walk," Les said in an injured tone, sizing up Chris out of the periphery of his eye.

"Is this your headquarters?" Julie asked, realizing that Les was displeased by her friendship with Chris. "Could we see it?"

"It's kind of off limits, but I'll give you a general idea. You'll see it's not as plush as over there where the paying guests stay. There are sixteen of us in the bunkhouse, and we share a couple of showers. In the middle is the mess hall, and we get the leftovers from the food you lot eat over at the lodge. It's heaped up buffet style. We have to grab quick or go hungry."

Julie and Chris peeked into the stark interior of the staff bunkhouse, and someone in one of the Coral Island T-shirts came up behind them, asking, "You aren't staff, are you? This area of the island is restricted." He turned to Les. "Do you know these people, Donaldson?"

"Well, yes. At least, I know one of them."

"They'll have to keep to the tracks. Have you finished the equipment check?"

"Almost," Les said, looking humiliated.

"Let's move on," Chris suggested, pushing Julie before him.

"See you later," Julie called to Les.

"You know that bloke, I take it," Chris said.

"He's sort of a friend of the family. It was his idea that I come out to the island. He's in charge of some of the activities, like snorkeling. I hope we didn't get him in trouble."

"I gathered that it troubled him to see you with another chap," Chris said. "Unpleasant fellow, that other one."

"He must be the boss of the staff," Julie surmised.

"That fellow, Les, has designs on you, I'm afraid," Chris said, his eyes twinkling.

"It's only that he feels responsible for me," Julie said, uneasy that Chris had so quickly noticed Les's proprietary attitude. "Maybe I'd better go back to the beach. He's expecting me to go on the walk. I guess he wants to be the one who shows me the island.''

"You'll learn a lot more about it with him than you would with me," Chris said cheerfully. "I'll go back with you. I didn't know there was an official nature walk.'' They turned away from the forbidden path to the staff quarters and started back down the road. A large white heron flapped into a tree beside the trail, and a couple of dozen mottled, long-legged brown and beige birds with oversized down-curved beaks stalked along the rocks next to the shore.

"Whimbrels," Chris said. "We have those in Melbourne.''

"They look familiar," Julie said. "I think I've seen them on the California beaches.''

Returning to the lodge patio, they sat at a table on the restaurant patio, and Chris bought Julie a Coke. He told her about Melbourne, down at the southern end of Australia, where the climate and vegetation was very different from the balmy, tropical scene on Coral Island. "It's only a hop, skip and a jump from there to Antarctica,'' he said.

Then Julie told Chris about the variety of climates and scenery in California, and Chris said he'd come backpacking over there some day.

Someone had set out a broken coconut on the ground, and a couple of tiny birds perched on either side of a half of it, pecking at the meat. Julie and Chris laughed as the coconut rocked comically back and forth in rhythm with the pecking of the birds. Chris had a camera around his neck, and he took a picture, crouching down on the ground. Then he took a picture of Julie.

"I can tell my friends I met a California girl," he said. "I once heard a song with that name.''

Just as Chris was snapping Julie's picture, Les arrived at the terrace. His face clouded in annoyance that Julie was still in Chris's company. A middle-aged man approached Les. "Is this where we meet for the eleven o'clock nature walk?" he asked.

"This is it," Les answered. "We'll wait until we're sure everyone is here."

A group of some twenty people assembled, and Les led them down the same path Julie and Chris had begun. Trees, shrubs, and insects were pointed out and identified. Les showed them a large nutmeg tree where dozens of flying foxes hung sleeping. They would waken at nightfall to forage for food. They saw the coarse stick nests of reef herons high in the canopy of the forest, and Les pointed out the red-crowned fruit pigeons, with their markings of lilac, yellow and green. Several parts of the island were barricaded, Les explained, for erosion control. New plants struggled to root themselves in sand dunes, and some sections of the shore had been sandbagged against the constant wearing as the tides pulled at the sand and wore down the limestone of the reef.

Although Les attempted to present his spiel on the features of the island in a smooth, professional manner, Julie could sense he was distracted by Chris, who hung closely beside her and frequently made some comment to her. On the opposite side of the beach from the lodge, the sugar-white sand stretched away undisturbed by sunbathers. A few stark, bleached remnants of trees protruded picturesquely, and Chris asked Julie to pose against one to take her picture.

"We have to move on," Les told him, scowling, although he had not objected when other members of the party stopped to snap photographs. Les had taken an obvious dislike to Chris. Yes, he was definitely jealous. It gave Julie a funny feeling—she who had so recently been dumped by the only guy she had ever really known well. But Les had no need to worry about Chris, for in a couple of hours, he'd be gone, hitchhiking to a place with the weird name of Yungaburra, he had told her. Yet it made her feel important to have such a guy as Les jealous of her. The image of Mike floated through her consciousness. He was bumming across the world just as Chris was. Probably he was striking up casual acquaintances like hers and Chris's. It didn't seem important, and Mike's memory bleached away in the blaze of sun off the coral shore.

"I wonder if we could drop out of the nature walk and just sit here on one of these logs and watch the ocean," Chris suggested. Les was about to lead the group back through the forest. "It's so deserted here, such unspoiled nature. This is the kind of place I like."

"I'd better stick with the nature walk," Julie told him. "Les was sort of appointed to show me around the island, and my dad expects me to stay with him."

"Lucky Les," Chris said. "Are you sure he's a trustworthy chaperone? It's not exactly with a protective eye that he looks at you. It would be my guess that he's envious of me for walking with you. I do wish our acquaintance were not to be so short. I could work on giving your friend something to be jealous about. But what can a bloke do when he has only an hour or two?"

Chris talked in a bantering tone, and Julie knew that he wasn't serious. Perhaps that was why she felt relaxed around Chris, where Les made her feel tense.

They continued on the nature walk, with Les turning around often to see what was going on between herself and Chris. Les looked particularly disturbed when he saw her giving Chris her address so he could send her copies of the snapshots he'd taken of her.

When they arrived back at the terrace and Les's charges began to disperse, he was able to concentrate his attention on Julie. He drew her aside, away from Chris.

"Who is this chap? He sticks to you like a leech. I'm not sure your father would like for you to take up with strangers, Julie," Les said. The controlled voice with which he had lectured the tourists fragmented into a frustrated sputter.

"He's just a guy traveling alone, and we got to talking. He's from Melbourne, and he's only here for the day. Be nice to him. You'll like him."

"Oh, he's only a day visitor?" Les's frown smoothed away. "He'll be leaving on the 3:30 boat then? I hope you don't mind my interfering. Your father entrusted you to my care, and I feel responsible. There are rascals in Australia, as anywhere else, and I wouldn't want you to..."

"Oh, Les, Chris is no rascal. He's a nice guy. Interesting, but alone. You ought to get acquainted and give him some pointers on where he should go next, after he leaves Coral Island, I mean. He's backpacking, just bumming around."

"Sorry if I've been stuffy," Les said. "If I only had more time to spend with you, I wouldn't be worried about your getting involved with some strange chap."

Julie laughed. "Involved? I just walked partway around the island and had a cup of coffee with him. That's minimum involvement. Don't worry about me. I've known a few guys before. I can handle myself." That was something of an exaggeration. Julie had been out with one guy—Mike.

"I don't want to be too protective, but your dad expects me to..."

"Quit apologizing, Les. And don't be hostile to Chris." She led Les back to her transient friend.

"So Julie tells me you're from Melbourne," Les said self-consciously. A little of his resentment toward the visitor still showed.

"I'm hungry after that walk," Julie said.

"It is lunchtime," Les said. "Unfortunately, I have to eat at staff quarters and then get ready for snorkeling instructions—which of course, will involve you, Julie. I can sit with you out here for about ten minutes before I have to go."

A scent of grilling hamburgers wafted about the terrace. "Just like home," Julie said happily, looking down the list of burgers. She ordered something called "Hamburger with the lot."

"They gave me the wrong thing," she exclaimed, startled, when her sandwich arrived. "This is an eggburger."

"That's what you ordered," Les said. "'The lot' includes an egg."

"Wow!" Julie said. "And it includes a lot more unexpected trimmings. I never saw a hamburger with beets before."

Les and Chris laughed at Julie's reaction to the Australian version of hamburgers, and then they became friendly. Les told Chris where he might travel in northern Queensland. "There's Lake Barrine, and also an ancient crater which has a waterfall with a swimming pool at its base. If you get over to Tam O'Shanter forest, you might run into a cassowary."

"After I've seen the sights in Queensland, I'm going on to the Northern Territory," Chris told Les. "I want to see some of those rock paintings the aborigines made."

Les had to return to staff quarters to eat. "Meet me here for the snorkeling session in an hour and fifteen minutes," he instructed Julie. He seemed less reluctant to leave Julie with Chris now that he knew Chris would soon leave the island.

Chris and Julie finished their lunch and wandered around the island, looking in on a crocodile museum where the huge reptiles dozed, looking unreal. Then Julie had to leave to meet the snorkeling class.

"Would you mind if I wrote you a postcard or something? I've never known anyone from America before," Chris said.

"I'd really like to know whether you made it all around Australia and back to Melbourne," Julie said. "I already gave you my address."

Julie went back to the terrace, the usual meeting place for the guides and activities people to meet the groups they were to lead and instruct. Another of the staff members was going to do a botanical tour of the island. Les had nine people, including herself, who wanted to learn to snorkel.

Chapter Six

Les led his group to an inlet which was roped off and provided calm, deep water. "This is the nearest thing to a swimming pool we have on Coral Island," he explained. Everyone sat on the rocks, dangling their feet. "Is there anyone here who can't swim?" he asked. They looked at one another and laughed.

"How many of you have passed a swimming test?" he asked.

"I have," Julie said. "I would have made the swim team at school except that I got an infected ear. It's all well now, and my doctor said I could swim again, but it kept me off the team."

"Tough," Les said. Five others said they'd passed the tests, and the remainder had to take them then and there, while the others looked on. "You should never dive unless you're a competent swimmer," Les explained. He made them swim freestyle 300 meters, and demonstrate the backstroke and the sidestroke. In addition, they had to tread water for a minute and float for five minutes. One thirtyish lady named Zelda couldn't pass the test, and Les said she'd have to work on it longer and try again after the snorkeling session. Meanwhile, he passed out masks, snorkels and fins to the others.

"Tomorrow we'll be going to the outer reef, where we can see a tremendous variety of undersea life," he told them, "and I want you all to be competent snorkelers so you won't miss anything."

They tested their masks, to be sure they were watertight. Julie pushed her hair out of the way and clamped the mask over her eyes and nose, taking a deep breath, as Les had instructed. The mask stayed on.

"Now check the nose pocket," Les said. "If you dive to inspect a fish or a coral and you feel pressure on your ears, you'll have to pinch your nostrils to clear the ears. Let's try it. Everybody, give your nose a pinch and then blow." Julie felt her ears pop. The last of the pressure inequality from the airplane ride was gone.

"Let me explain about pressure," Les said. Julie admired his easy, knowledgeable poise. "Did you realize that all your life you've been walking around with almost fifteen pounds of pressure on every square inch of your body? That's how much the atmosphere weighs. Now, suppose you're out snorkeling and you see some interesting gorge full of fantastic marine life. You dive down thirty-three feet to have a look. Now, you'll have about thirty pounds of pressure per inch weighing on you. That added pressure could have an effect. For instance, face masks have been known to squeeze so hard against divers' faces that they come out with black or bloodshot eyes."

The prospective snorkelers looked at one another with exaggerated expressions of horror.

"Go down to sixty-six feet, and the pressure is three times as much as normal," Les continued. "But when we dive that deep, we're into more advanced diving, probably with an Aqualung. We won't be going down beyond the thirty-three foot level with our snorkels."

"I should hope not," one of a couple of girls who seemed to be friends, said. "If I came back from my vacation with a black eye, what would people say?" The two girls, Wendy and Louise, wore very skimpy bathing suits. In fact, Julie observed that the Australians exposed a lot more skin on the beach than she'd noticed in Northern California.

The others in the snorkeling group were a married couple in their twenties, who introduced themselves as Arnold and Freida, and a couple of brothers, Brian, about Les's age, and Will, fourteen, who had received the trip to Coral Island as a birthday present. Then there was a fortyish guy, Al Green. The lady who had trouble swimming, they later found out, was from New Zealand. She was paddling frantically, looking now and then toward Les, as though she expected a lot of help. Wendy and Louise listened admiringly to Les, as though they thought he was attractive.

Now he was describing how to fit the snorkel onto the left side of the the face mask and to grip the mouthpiece with the teeth. "Hold the flange between the front of your teeth and your lip," he instructed. Julie found that an awkward position.

"I thought these snorkels were supposed to have ping pong balls at the top to keep the water from getting into your mouth," somebody said.

"Those snorkels we don't approve," Les said, frowning. "Don't worry about a little water getting into your mouth. I'll show you how to blow it out if your snorkel gets submerged. But first, let's get our fins on. I always like to put my fins on in the water so I don't trip over the flaps and break a leg."

"Sounds like a hazardous pastime we're taking up," Al Green said.

"Not really," Les said. "Incidentally, the best way to walk in fins is backward. Now, everybody in, and get those fins on. Remember, this isn't a tiled swimming pool. This inlet has been dredged out a bit for training, but there's still coral on the bottom, and it can cut."

The swimmers eased themselves into the waist deep water with their fins and tried standing on one leg to slip the fin on the other foot. "Here, let me get that," Les said to Julie. "Lean on me. Slide your foot into the flipper and then pull it up." Wendy looked resentfully at Julie as she dropped her fin in the water and had to fish around for it with no assistance from Les.

"Am I getting any closer to passing?" Zelda called in a petulant voice. "I can't possibly get this back stroke without some help."

"I'm busy with the snorkelers right now, Ma'am," Les said. "After they get their basic instruction and can move around with their gear on, I'll get to you."

"Busy with his girlfriend," Louise commented in an audible whisper.

"When we're snorkeling in the open water, we use the buddy system," Les said, ignoring the remark. "Never dive alone. Have someone watching you in case you get in trouble. Let's see, you two are together," he indicated the two girls. "And you, Arnold and Freida, can look after each other, and then the brothers. You," he told Al Green, "can pair up with the lady from New Zealand when she gets checked out."

"How about me?" Julie asked.

"You and I will be buddies," Les said. The lady from New Zealand sniffed, and Wendy and Louise raised eyebrows at one another. Julie feared Les was arousing resentment in the rest of the group by paying too much attention to her. Even if she was a friend of the family, shouldn't he treat her impersonally when he was instructing a class? It embarrassed her, and she thought it would have been more suitable to assign her as a buddy to Al Green, while he took Zelda, who would obviously need a lot of watching.

"When we're underwater," Les went on, apparently oblivious of the undercurrent among the snorkelers, "of course, we can't talk to our partners, so we communicate with them by hand signals. Suppose you see something out to the left you want to investigate. Just get your partner's attention and then point in the direction you want your buddy to follow. Now and then, give the signal to your partner that everything is all right with you." Les held up his hand with his thumb and forefinger joined in an "O". "On the other hand, if you're having some kind of trouble, swivel your hand downward from the wrist so your buddy can come to your aid. Suppose you see a school of jellyfish approaching, and you want to warn your mate away. Put up your hand with your palm facing him, like a stop signal. If you're in real trouble, like your foot's caught in the jaws of a giant clam or a shark is after you, give your partner the distress signal, with your hand in a fist, moving back and forth from the elbow." Les had the swimmers repeat all the signals until they had them memorized.

"I'm only joking about the hazards," he reassured them. "I've never known anyone to be chased by a shark out here, and as you'll see the giant clams move rather too ponderously to take a bite of a foot."

Then it was time to submerge. Julie peered through the mask with her face down in the water. What she saw astonished her. Who would believe that under the water there was a completely different world from what one was accustomed to seeing? A fat striped black and yellow fish swam into view against a wall of weird and beautiful shapes and colors. Fronds waved and tossed in the gentle current, worm-like creatures with flower-shaped noses undulated, and a mass of silvery minnows darted in unison beneath her mask and disappeared behind a stony branch of dead coral.

Julie surfaced with a gasp of delight. "Is that the first time you've looked into the sea?" Les asked.

"I've been swimming underwater a little, at Lake Tahoe," she said, "but without a mask, and I couldn't really see anything. I just saw a huge black and yellow fish."

"He might not have been as large as you thought," Les said. The rest of the group came up for air, and Les told them all, "When you're looking through your mask, objects appear larger than they really are. So don't be alarmed if you see a giant fish quite near to you. He's not as big as he looks, and he's also farther away."

Zelda complained that she was missing out, she had no equipment. Les grudgingly gave her a mask and snorkel and said she could look, but he wasn't going to check her out to go to the outer reef until she had demonstrated swimming proficiency. "Now you just watch while I finish up with the group," he told her impatiently. Julie could tell Les wished the lady from New Zealand would get lost.

"We'll go down now to learn how to clear the snorkel tube," he said. "Your masks are all on, your snorkel tubes are in place. Now I want you to put your faces in the water, hold your tongue against your teeth to seal off your mouth, take a breath, and then submerge to about an arm's length. You'll find out that water can fill your tube, and then you'll come up and blow that water out as you exhale."

They practiced this maneuver several times, sending spouts of spray above the surface like so many whales. Once Julie swallowed some salt water. Les told her she hadn't given a strong enough puff to shoot the water out. He gave her a drink of fresh water to rinse the salt from her mouth.

Then they had instructions on how to fin. Once Les had impressed them with the correct technique, he asked them to practice finning and breathing while he worked with Zelda.

Julie began to feel comfortable in the snorkeling gear. She pretended she was a frog, experiencing the power the fins gave her to shoot through the water. She worked for a smooth rhythm, coordinating her breathing and finning. Although Les was working with Zelda, he continued to observe Julie. She knew, because once he came over to tell her to point her toes down a little more.

"Try finning on your back," he said. "You won't need your snorkel for that. She enjoyed finning while lying on the water looking upward to see sea birds wheeling out from the island. Seeming to forget about Zelda, Les taught Julie the dolphin kick, with both fins together, and then he turned her gently on her side. "If you get tired, try finning this way." His hands lingered about her waist.

Zelda looked on critically. "I thought you were supposed to be teaching me the backstroke?"

"I see that you were privileged to learn some special techniques," Wendy said when she and Louise surfaced.

"I was just finning on my back, and on my side. Here, I'll show you, it's fun." She wanted to be friends with everyone in the group so that they wouldn't resent Les's extra attention to her.

When Les had finished the allotted hour and a half of snorkeling instruction, he said to Julie: "I'll have to work on this lady a little more to see if I can get her up to par. She insists she wants to swim in the outer reef. But would you stay around so I can walk back with you?"

Julie didn't want to watch the incompetent swimmer flounder about in the water, so she walked along the shore. It was low tide, and what had looked like ocean an hour or two ago had emerged into a wide expanse of alternating puddles and coral outcroppings. Julie walked through the puddles and patches of sand. Being aware that the coral had live polyps on top, she didn't want to walk on them. She saw a mollusk moving through a shallow pool and crouched down to watch as the oval-shaped, mottled brown and white shell swayed above the jelly-like mantle foot of the animal.

Julie started when a hand touched her bare shoulder. She looked up to see Les bending beside her. "What are you so intent on?" he asked, poking the shell until it withdrew its foot. "It's a red-mouthed olive. A good specimen."

"I'm afraid to walk out farther," Julie said. "All of these rocks are alive."

"Right. I should have warned you. We usually don't go fossicking in our bare feet. You can get a nasty cut from sharp coral. You can also step on a poisonous shell. A cone, for instance. There are also killer stone fish that very much resemble a piece of rock."

"Fossicking?"

"That's our term for walking on an exposed coral fringe when the tide is out. You ought to wear tennis shoes or boots."

Les looked at Julie affectionately and changed the subject. "You did very well on your snorkeling today," he said. "You'll be ready to enjoy the sights on the outer reef tomorrow."

"What about the lady from new Zealand? Did you finish with her?"

"She's about finished me off. She's the sort of person who shouldn't sign up for water sports, because she isn't really an experienced swimmer. She insists on going out tomorrow, but I have a feeling she's going to be a constant problem. Maybe I can persuade her to ride in the glass-bottom boat."

"Everyone else in your group was competent," Julie reminded him.

"Especially you," Les said in a caressing voice that excited Julie and yet made her uneasy. She'd only known Les for two days. "I wish I could hang around out here with you for a while," he said, "but unfortunately, I'm on duty. I have to collect all the equipment and get it back to staff headquarters. Come on, we'll at least get to walk back together."

Julie helped him gather up the fins, masks and snorkels and put them in a large bag which he slung over his back. All the other snorkelers had wandered off to various points around the island. Julie and Les cut through one of the forest paths surrounded by a tangle of vines, low-growing palms, tall trees and tropical shrubs.

Julie started to mention to Les that maybe he'd given her too much of his attention, so much that the others in the snorkeling group had felt neglected. Then she decided not to. He might resent her telling him how to conduct his business.

A couple of girls called to Les as he walked by. It was obvious that he was exposed to lots of attractive young girls on the island. Julie could see them lying about on the sand in their skimpy bikinis. She glanced at Les's bronzed muscles and sun-bleached hair and brows. No wonder so many female sunbathers turned to watch him as he walked by. Julie couldn't believe he was really interested in her. It was just an act he was accustomed to playing. The staff guys on Coral

Island were obviously chosen for their looks and charm, and he'd no doubt thrilled many island visitors by walking down this same path with them. Julie determined not to take him too seriously.

As they approached Leslie's quarters, Julie saw the same man who had chased her and Chris away from the staff compound. He gave Julie a critical once-over and looked at his watch. "Your snorkeling session ran overtime, Donaldson," he stated flatly.

"Sorry, Neil. One of the participants was a very rusty swimmer. I had to spend some time bringing her up to par. No, it wasn't Julie," he added, when Neil cast a questioning glance at her. "She's first-rate."

"Well, get your gear checked in," Neil said, turning abruptly from Julie.

"I'll see you over at the lodge for tea at four," Les said in a low voice to Julie.

She walked away, feeling lonely. She needed more of Les's time than these few snatched moments. She thought of phoning her dad. Then she rejected that idea. Not on her first day away, when he thought she was so ready to be independent. She tried to imagine where he was: in the hotel room? interviewing someone?

Everyone she passed was a stranger, which only made her feel more alone. Over by the lodge there was a gift shop. She wandered in, intending to buy a few postcards to send home, and was sidetracked by a rack of coverups with Great Barrier Reef fish hand-painted down the front. Her dad had given her some cash, and although buying the coverup would almost deplete her money supply, she couldn't resist. She added a few postcards to her purchase, and rushed to her room. She'd wear the new dress when she went to tea, and she'd appear to be a reef dweller, instead of a conspicuous American.

Julie sat at the table outside her cabin and wrote postcards. One to Mom, with a picture of the coral gardens; a scary picture of a spotted ray for Harlan, and a school of pale blue fish with yellow stripes for Kim. "Guess what?" she wrote on the card to Kim. "It turned out that Leslie is not a girl, but a very smashing guy who is teaching me to snorkel." Should she send a postcard to Mike? She tried to imagine him on his bike up in Canada, but he seemed remote and indistinct. A tall, skinny redheaded guy in plaid shorts walked by her cabin and said "G'day," and Julie repeated the Australian greeting. She looked at her watch. It was almost teatime. Stuffing her postcards in her purse, she hurried toward the lodge, realizing that she was impatient for Les's company.

Several lodge guests, including the two girls in Julie's snorkeling group, Wendy and Louise, were already at tea. The staff people, freshly dressed in their white socks, shorts and shirts, were mingling with the guests. There was a small nature library in the corner of the room, and Les was showing the girls a book describing the shells of the reef. When Julie entered the room, he shoved the book toward one of the girls.

"Excuse me," he said, making a beeline for Julie, and grabbing her by both hands. "Where have you been? I was afraid you'd fallen asleep again." His eyes bathed her face with a radiant smile. Les's vitality and enthusiasm touched a chord of pleasure in Julie, and drew a matching smile from her. Les tucked her hand under his arm and covered it with his hand. He took her about the room introducing her to the other staff members.

"I promised your dad I'd introduce you to a female staff member," he said, approaching a tall girl with large dark eyes and a swatch of long black hair which she tossed alternately over one shoulder and then the other. "Rana here is our island botanist. She can tell you what every plant on the island is. She usually leads the nature walk. The rest of us just fill in now and then."

"You're an American," Rana stated. "I heard that Les was deeply involved with someone from overseas." Rana's eyes twinkled teasingly.

"I promised Julie's dad she'd meet some other women over here on the island," Les said. "Mr. Blacker is a sort of business acquaintance of my father."

"Great to have you on the island, Julie," Rana said, looking teasingly from her to Les.

Kevin, whom Les introduced as a fellow diving instructor, cautioned Julie, "Beware of this chap." His twinkly blue eyes flashed mischievously toward Les. "He's about as trustworthy as a barracuda."

"I thought you were my friend," Les said, returning the playful sparkle. "Come on, Julie, let's get away from my detractors."

"Wait a minute, aren't you going to introduce me to your guest?" Neil asked, displaying the same brusqueness with which he'd dismissed Julie and Chris earlier.

"Oh, Neil! Julie Blacker. And this is Neil McAndrews, our staff director."

"I saw you this morning on the other side of the island," Julie reminded him.

"Sorry about that!" Neil said, not smiling. "But we have to maintain some rules and regulations."

The staff people dispersed to talk to the guests then. Some of the other snorkelers from Les's group had arrived, and Les arranged for them to share a table at dinner, so that Julie wouldn't be dining alone.

"I wish I weren't so tied up with my job," he said. "I'd like to be with you all the time, Julie. By the way, don't let Neil bother you. That's just the way he is—abrasive."

"I don't think he likes me."

"He treats everyone the same. Thinks the staff should be on duty twenty-four hours a day. Of course, part of our duty is being hospitable to the guests, but evidently he doesn't feel my hospitality to you is sufficiently superficial. He's guessed that my interest in you goes deeper, that I'm not just doing the job or putting on an act." They had gone out through the overhanging palms to the terrace. They faced the setting sun which shimmered a fiery path across the placid sea. "It's true, Julie. You've quite captured my heart. I think of you constantly. It's an agony to have you on the island and to be apart from you."

Julie stiffened with surprise at this declaration. "I'm just a novelty," she said, trying to sound offhanded and flippant. "You'll soon grow tired of me."

"Small chance. Remember when I picked you up after you'd fallen asleep at our barbecue?"

"That was excruciatingly embarrassing."

"To me it was very pleasant. You were so soft and light, I knew then I couldn't go out to the island without you. I had to persuade your father to let you come with me."

Les's directness and intensity were rather scary to Julie. Mike had never come out with such a statement, especially when she first knew him. Was Les just a smooth talker? Why her? There was no lack of girls on the island. Why were people always warning her about Les? She remembered Jane's comment, "Come into my parlor, said the spider to the fly." And just now, Kevin had advised her, "Beware of this chap." Les seemed to have a reputation as a ladies' man. His arm was draped about her shoulder as they stood on that impossibly romantic terrace, watching flights of birds wheel against the setting sun. His hand caressed her upper arm, and she moved away from him, whirling toward the door to the lodge. "I want to look at some of the books before dinner," she said. "We'll be seeing all these fish and coral tomorrow, and I'd like to recognize them."

Chapter Seven

Julie was conscious of Les following her closely as she entered the lodge. Others seemed to be noticing, too. Not knowing what book she picked out of the shelf, she opened it, looking blindly at a page, feeling the proximity of Les.

"Julie," she heard Les's soft, pleading voice beside her. She felt penned in, suffocated. "I have so little time to spend with you. Let's not waste it."

"People are noticing. That guy, Neil, is watching us."

"Let them, and him, too. They've seen people attracted to one another before."

"Les, you have to cool it. We don't know each other that well. You told my dad you were going to teach me about life on the reef. Now that I want to learn about it, you're putting me off."

"You're the one who's putting me off. Can't you see I've fallen in love with you, Julie."

There were too many people around. Julie couldn't react in such a crowd. "That's weird," she said. "You're imagining it."

"It's real," he insisted, his eyes riveted to hers.

"This is no place to talk about something private like that, with everyone listening." She was shocked. Mike had never said he'd fallen in love with her, even when they were going steady last year.

"That's why I tried to talk to you alone on the terrace, but you ran away. Julie, I'll have to go to dinner with the staff people, and after that, I have to show the movie on the history of the reef. Afterward, we'll meet and talk. There won't be anyone around to interfere."

Les was too agitated to tell her about the fish now, and the pictures blurred before her eyes. She wasn't sure she could handle someone who had declared himself to be in love. She didn't want him to be in love with her, and she dreaded meeting him after the movie.

After a while all the staff people went to their community dinner. Julie and the others from the snorkeling group sat at a table together. Julie looked blindly at the menu, and while the others were deciding what to order, Al Green, the fortyish man, addressed in a bantering tone, "Young lady, it looks as if you've made a conquest of our snorkeling instructor!"

"Not really," Julie said in a flustered voice. "His dad and mine are friends, and he's just supposed to be showing me part of Australia."

"Just our luck to get in a group with that young man who's too distracted to give us the proper attention. We all might drown while he's showing you Australia," Zelda said.

"We'll be out in open water tomorrow, diving off a boat," Wendy said. "Maybe you'd better share him a little."

"We're all new to this," Louise added.

"Not me," Brian, the older of the two brothers, contradicted. "I've been out here before. Will has been begging me to bring him out ever since he was eight years old. We're from Alice Springs, practically in the middle of Australia, and as landlocked as you can be. Will has never seen the ocean before."

"We're utter novices, Freida and I," Arnold said, smiling at his wife.

"Are you two on your honeymoon?" Al Green asked. He seemed to enjoy putting people on the spot. Julie was glad to have the focus of the conversation shift away from her. She disliked being conspicuous.

"In a manner of speaking, you might say we are, although our wedding was last December. We put the honeymoon off until the dry season, although we're not, actually, what you'd call newlyweds." He turned and smiled again at Freida.

Julie ordered barramundi, a kind of fish that was supposed to be very special in the vicinity of the reef. After dinner, Al asked, "Is everybody going to the movie? Let's walk over together."

There was only a small crowd at the showing, which was held under the stars on an open part of the terrace. Les was threading the movie reel into a projector, and when he saw Julie approaching, he got the film tangled and left it dangling from the machine while he rushed to pull out a chair for her. Then he tackled the film again, seemingly all thumbs. Eventually he got the documentary under way. Julie could see the members of their group smirking at one another over the incident.

Les announced that the film was a history of the reef, and the projector began to whir. The audience heard about Captain James Cook who had been sailing up the eastern coast of Australia in 1770, unaware that the thousand-mile Great Barrier Reef existed. After sailing past Cairns, Captain Cook was jolted into acquaintance with the reef when his ship ran against the coral heads, was damaged, and had to go ashore for repairs at a point later named after the captain, Cooktown. As other ships, including the *Bounty* of the famous mutiny, sailed in the waters around the reef, many of them crashing as Captain Cook had, the extent of the huge coral formation became evident. It was mapped and its depths explored.

Julie was astonished to hear that when navigators had first landed on the idyllic Coral Island, they had been attacked by aborigines, and on many other cays and islands of the reef, sailors attempting to land had been killed by cannibals.

The film described the activities that developed through the years of the reef's history: pearl fishing, a sea cucumber drying factory, the establishment of wildlife sanctuaries and of research stations for the study of undersea ecology. The film ended with breathtaking scenes of the coral gardens beneath the water.

"Tomorrow we'll be down there seeing it all for ourselves," Brian said.

"When do we leave for our snorkeling trip?" Wendy asked.

"We'll meet on the pier at ten o'clock," Les told her. The audience drifted away from the movie into the tropical night that was scented with the heavy perfume of plumeria blossoms.

"I'll be finished winding this reel in a moment, Julie," Les said. He rewound the film while another staff member took down the screen and stacked the folding chairs. "Would you take the film and projector back to storage?" he asked his co-worker. "I've got a heavy date."

Les's colleague cast a speculative look at Julie, which gave her a clandestine feeling. She didn't like the sound of the word "heavy."

While Les and his friend were getting the film in its container and the projector ready to transport, Julie thought of her dad. How could her dad have put her into such a position? Why hadn't he acted as he might have at home? He had suddenly stepped out of character and without any hesitation just unsnapped the leash from his only daughter and sent her out alone to this romantic island with a good-looking, amorous Aussie. She felt a sudden stab of anger toward her dad. Her mom and Harlan had expected him to be supervising her, and he had washed his hands of her, just left her defenseless.

"Let's take a walk down the beach," Les suggested. "All day I've thought of nothing except the moment when I'd be off duty and I could be with you."

"You've been with me a lot today," she said, wishing to squelch any notion Les had of being anything more than friendly.

"Not half as much as I wished for, which was every minute."

"I thought you loved your job so much that you couldn't leave it."

"Here, we'll follow this track to the beach." Les took her elbow in his hand to guide her toward the ocean. Julie feared his touch, so she said, "I'll race you," and shook him off, flying along the path until she reached the sand. The three-quarters moon cast a pale light over the landscape, fashioning fantastic shadows from the palm trees. She wanted to be with him, yet she feared to be. This was different from her dates with Mike. Mike was not so impulsive, so physical or as emotional and persistent as Les. Mike had been younger when she went with him. Her parents had imposed limits on Mike which he had always observed. Maybe that was why he'd dumped her once he met college girls who were out from under parental rules, as she was now, suddenly cast adrift from her father.

Julie sped down the beach with Les sprinting after her. She could see the ghostly shapes of herons roosting in the trees. "Julie, wait," he called, accelerating his pace until at last he caught her and held her captive against him. "Why do you keep running away from me? Don't you realize that this is the first time we've been alone together? First there were our parents and then all these island visitors that kept us from talking to one another."

Julie extricated herself from Les's arms. She thought about her dad, who was probably asleep right now in that same room where they'd discussed her visit to the island. What was it he'd said? Something about keeping the family's rules even when they weren't around. Something about the trip to the island being a test of how she could handle independence.

It was going to be too hard a test, with someone like Les—appealing, determined, affectionate, intense. That intensity was what made him so hard to handle. He ought to lighten up. She forced a laugh that was supposed to be carefree, but it came out nervous and shrill.

"You're not taking me seriously, Julie," he said. "I started to tell you this afternoon at tea. I love you. It began as soon as you stepped into the airport lobby, and the more I've seen of you, the more that feeling has grown."

"Leslie Donaldson, you're crazy," Julie said. "You don't know very much about me. You seem to fall in love very easily. You probably meet too many girls out here on Coral Island. Those two in our snorkeling group, for instance. I can tell they would welcome more of your time. They've been rather snippy to me because you've been giving me all your attention, being my undersea buddy, for instance.''

"Don't you understand, Julie? I give you all that attention because I can't keep my mind off you. I wish those two girls and the other members of our group weren't even there.''

"You teach these groups week after week. Don't tell me you don't find girls among them that you fall for. To say nothing of the cute staff members you've been working with all summer. That redhead who brought the towels into my cabin, for instance. You probably know her a lot better than you know me.''

Les was on the defensive now. "You don't believe or trust me,'' he complained. "If I had been attracted to the staff girls, wouldn't I be with one of them now? I wouldn't even have suggested you come out here. Can't you see? I thought you were a special person who would like the same things I do. I wanted to share the coral gardens with you so you could experience the same excitement I feel when I dive.''

A hurt quality had entered Les's voice and Julie began to feel sorry for him. "Calm down, Leslie,'' she said. "I can't wait to see the coral gardens. I'm really grateful that you invited me. Maybe it's true that I don't quite trust you. It's pretty unusual for me to be by myself so far from my family. I really do like you a lot, in fact. I think you're pretty terrific. Only I haven't known you long enough for you to start talking about love.''

"I'm rushing you, that's it. I've scared you.'' A tender one replaced the aggrieved quality of his voice. "Maybe you do agitate my hormones, Julie, but don't worry, I know how to conduct myself around a proper young lady. You don't need to fear on that score. But do you believe in instant attraction? That's what I felt for you. I love the way your hair curls up like feathers, and the shape of your eyes, so round and wondering. I want them to see my favorite things. No, I don't know you very well, Julie. You're deliciously mysterious to me, and I want to know more.''

''You're a puzzle to me, too, Les. Tell me more about yourself.''

''You know all about me. You've been in the house where I've spent my whole life. You've met my parents and sister and her friends. You've seen me in action on my job. You know what my ambitions are. What more is there to know?''

Les and Julie were sitting on a pile of sandbags that had been stacked along a portion of the shore in danger of eroding. They had a view of the moon-silvered sand of the curving beach. It was low tide. Out in the sea the fringing coral had emerged, glistening wetly in the weak celestial light.

''And another thing you know about me is that I'm in love with you.'' Julie was suddenly crushed against Les, the warmth of his lips on hers. The pleasant shock of his kiss drove other thoughts from her mind. She relaxed in his arms, lulled by his embrace.

Then her alarm system took over, and she thought of her dad back in the hotel in Cairns. She needed to talk to him. Unaccustomed emotions had seized her, and she wasn't sure that she was as trustworthy as her dad imagined.

She wriggled from Les's arms, and he tried to capture her again. ''Les!'' she cried. ''We have to cool it.''

''Why?'' he asked. ''You love me, too. I can tell.''

Footsteps sounded somewhere near them. Les and Julie turned toward the sound. It was Freida and Arnold, emerging onto the beach from the track through the woods.

''Well!'' Arnold exclaimed. ''Someone else had the same idea we had, watching the sea in the moonlight. Mind if we join you?''

"Of course not," Julie said. Les ran his hand through his hair, looking disgruntled.

"I hope you're enjoying the island," he said in his formal, staff voice.

"We are!" Freida said enthusiastically. "We can hardly wait for our trip out into the ocean tomorrow. Arnold and I went back to the lodge after the movie and studied the book on coral. We'll be able to pick out all the different kinds. Branch coral, flange coral, brain coral—what a name! But it does look exactly like a brain."

Freida and Arnold talked on, revealing that Arnold was a sheep rancher and that they lived in the country, in New South Wales. They had known one another since childhood, and they were strangely alike, their facial reactions being almost identical, with toothsome smiles and crinkles around their eyes. They were of the same weathered coloration, medium height and slender body build. Julie had the impression that they seldom disagreed.

Les didn't have much to say. Now and then Julie could feel his hand caressing her arm. Julie tried to ask polite questions about sheep-raising, and at last she stood up. "I'm out of my time zone," she said, stifling a yawn, "and I don't think I can keep awake any longer."

"I'm feeling drowsy myself," Freida agreed. "We ranchers keep early hours, right, Arnold?"

"I'm ready to retire," Arnold said. They all turned toward the path through the forest. Les kept a moody silence as they approached the cabins, and they discovered that Freida and Arnold had the cabin next to Julie's. The cabins were connected by a wall.

Julie felt secure knowing that she'd made friends with the couple next door. There was someone she could call on in case of emergency. A kind of buffer between herself and Les's dangerous charm. Julie was relieved that the couple was there saying good-night and she could slip into her cabin without another of Les's unsettling kisses.

She fell asleep remembering over and over his declarations of love, and the warmth of his embrace. She decided she'd call her dad in the morning just to hear his voice and let him know she'd made it okay through the first day on Coral Island.

Freida knocked on her door the next morning to ask if she'd like to walk to breakfast with them. "You're quite alone here," Freida remarked. "Arnold and I were wondering how old you are, if you don't mind my asking. You seem very young."

"I'll be seventeen on my next birthday."

Arnold appeared from the next cabin. "This is the big day, when we submerge," he reminded them.

On the way over, Julie explained to them how she happened to be traveling alone. She stopped at the phone booth outside the lodge. "I want to call my dad before breakfast," she said. "Otherwise, he'll be gone and I won't reach him."

The sound of her dad's voice sent a delicious flood of relief through Julie. His voice was big, confident, reassuring, substantial. "Daddy," she said. "I just wanted to know if you were okay. I was afraid you might be getting lonely."

"I've missed you, honey, but I've been busy. I was just about to set out for an interview with some shipping people."

"I'm doing great, Dad. I've learned to dive with a snorkel, and in a couple of hours we're going out to see the coral gardens."

"Wonderful, baby. I knew you'd have a good time, and that you're being well taken care of over there."

"I've met this couple from New South Wales. They have the room next to mine." She thought he'd like to hear that. "They'll be snorkeling with me today."

"Good. I'm glad you're making friends."

"The island is beautiful. Are you coming out this weekend?"

"I've made arrangements to come out on Friday in the late afternoon. We won't be coming on the morning trip. One of the Donaldsons' friends will bring us out by motorboat. It will only take a few minutes."

"You said 'us,'" Julie observed.

"You've discovered my surprise. Jane and her boyfriend are coming along. Jane will bunk with you and Richard with me. Then we'll all come back on Sunday afternoon."

"Terrific, Dad. I have to go to breakfast or I'll miss the boat. See you on Friday, if I don't call you before." Julie hurried to breakfast, bolstered by the hearty sound of her dad's voice.

Some of the others had finished and were already on their way down the pier. The catamaran from the mainland appeared on the horizon. Leslie appeared soon after the group had assembled. He carried a bag filled with snorkeling equipment over his shoulder.

"Everyone ready to dive?" he asked in his cheerful, official staff voice, but he didn't look at everyone. He singled out Julie, his eyes locking on hers in a way that made her wary.

The catamaran docked and let out its load of passengers to Coral Island, while Les's group joined those that remained on board to view the undersea life on the outer reef.

"There must be a hundred people here," Julie exclaimed. "We'll bump into one another's snorkels."

"Very few of these people are going out to dive," Les explained. "Most of them will just view the reef from glass-bottom boats or a little sub they have out here."

"Could I have my mask now?" Will, the younger of the two brothers asked. "I want to be ready to go under the sea right away after we arrive."

"You have plenty of time. It takes a while to get to the outer reef," Les said. He told them that the ship's pilot had to go through one of the few safe passages through the maze of coral to get to the other side of the reef. "Let's hope the sea is clear today," he added. "Last week, a storm out at sea stirred up the water, and it was so murky the diving was bad. We could only see a few feet in front of our masks, and some of our trips were canceled."

The catamaran passed out into the open water, and there was some turbulence. The craft rocked as though it were going over a washboard. Julie held onto the rail to keep her balance. Zelda wobbled and staggered from her seat on the open deck to confront Les.

"I think I'm getting seasick," she announced. "What should I do?"

"There's not much we can do about it now," Les replied. "If you knew you were prone to seasickness, you should have taken some Dramamine before you came, or had one of those antiseasick patches put behind your ear."

"But I've never been seasick before. I never knew you could get seasick on just a short trip. You might have warned us what we were in for." Her voice betrayed resentment at Les's unsympathetic attitude.

"I've heard that if you eat lemon drops, it will help," Julie said. "I have some Life Savers. Try one." Julie frowned at Les. He should be more helpful.

"Look," he said grudgingly to Zelda, noting Julie's disapproval. "Why don't you go inside and sit down and I'll send the hostess over to talk to you. She probably has sea-sick passengers every day. Might have something to give you."

The ailing passenger went inside, and Julie could see her holding her hand over her eyes. Les gave a high sign to one of the ship's two hostesses and pointed to Zelda.

"You could have been a little more sympathetic," Julie scolded.

"That woman is a royal pain. I'm not a doctor. I'm a snorkeling instructor. If she insists on diving with us, she's going to cause all kinds of problems. Why did she have to be in my group?"

"I guess she came out here to see what it looks like under the sea, just like the rest of us, and she doesn't want to miss out."

"I'm going to see if I can persuade her to go on the glass bottom boat or the sub, and get her off my conscience," Les said.

"You know, Les, you've been giving me too much atten-tion and shortchanging the rest of the group. I'm going to mingle around the ship and get acquainted with some other people, and I want you to go over and talk to Louise and Wendy, or Al, or Will and his brother. Act like you're at least interested in them."

"Julie, since I met you, I haven't been able to get inter-ested in anyone else."

"I don't want to hear about it, Leslie Donaldson. You have eight other people who are depending on you today, and I don't want to be the cause for your neglecting them."

Julie followed through on her plan of mixing among the passengers. She met people from Darwin, Sydney, Can-berra, New Zealand and Adelaide.

Chapter Eight

Help me round up our group," Les asked Julie. "We're almost to our destination."

Julie looked over the flat expanse of ocean toward the horizon. "I don't see anything."

"There's nothing on top of the water to see. It won't be visible until you're submerged," Les said.

"You mean we're just going to be sitting on the open ocean all day?"

"Not exactly." Les gave her a mysterious smile, his eyes sparkling with anticipation. "Anyway, let's see how many of our snorkelers you can find. They're scattered all over the ship. We'll meet here."

Julie went first to Zelda, who was still seated inside the craft with her eyes closed. She touched the woman lightly on the sleeve of her dark blue windbreaker. "How are you feeling?" she asked gently.

"That hostess didn't do a thing for me," she complained. "I don't know how I'm going to get through the rest of the day."

"We're about to drop anchor," Julie told her. "Les wants all of our group down by the gangplank."

"He should have warned me about the rough water."

"I'm sure you'll feel better when *The Dolphin* stops moving," Julie said. "Maybe if you come out and breathe some fresh air, you'll feel okay. Listen, you can hear the engines going off."

"We're stopping right in the middle of the ocean," Zelda said. "There's no place to go ashore."

"Les says that this is a submerged reef. We'll have to dive to see it. But anyway, the ship will be stationary for a while, so you're sure to feel better. Don't you want to come with me to meet the others?"

"I'll stay right where I am."

"I hope you'll be okay. I have to go now. I'm supposed to be rounding up the rest of the group."

"Young lady," Zelda took a parting shot as Julie turned to go, "if that instructor could keep his eyes off you, the whole group would benefit."

Julie didn't answer. So everyone noticed Les's infatuation. Maybe it was real, not just a line, an act. She wandered around the deck and found Louise talking to one of the ship's crew, a guy with a neatly trimmed mustache and such symmetrical eyebrows that he appeared artificial.

"We'll all meet down by the gangplank to get ready for diving," Julie said. "Les wants us all together."

"Maybe I'll run across you under the sea," the crewman said, smiling at Louise.

"At any rate, I'll see you on the way back," she responded, following Julie.

Will and Brian, the brothers, were hanging over the rail looking down into the sea when Julie found them.

"They say we've arrived at the reef, but we can't see anything," Will said.

"Come on down, and Les will explain it to you," Julie said. Brian and Will joined her and Louise. They went down the stairway to the lower deck. Les was waiting there with Wendy, Al, Arnold and Freida.

"We're all here except Zelda," Les said.

"She says she's still feeling queasy. She wants to stay on the ship," Julie told him.

Les looked exasperated. "I'll have to ask the hostess to keep an eye on her," he said. "She won't get anything out of sitting on the ship all day. Maybe she can be persuaded to go for a ride in the sub. It's very stable. Now, that leaves Al without a buddy. We'll make up a trio—Al, Julie and me. Wait here while I tell the hostess about Zelda."

When Les returned, he told them they'd be transported on the reef's glass bottom boat to a diving platform that was permanently anchored here. On the way out, he said, "I guess you noticed that all of you were required to sign on. That's to make sure we don't leave anyone out on the reef."

Brian laughed, and Les continued. "That may sound ridiculous, but it's really happened. Not on this reef, but down south, a load of passengers went out diving, and one of them was still out at departure time and got left behind on the reef at low tide. There wasn't any platform there, and when the tide came in, sharks and all, the abandoned passenger had to climb on the highest bommie—that's another name for coral head. Luckily, he found one that kept him above the water line until he was rescued the next day. Ever since then, the bommie has been known as Roughley's rock. You'll even find it on some maps. And ever since then, all the ships bringing people out to snorkel and dive have kept a roster of who's aboard, and won't leave until everyone has checked back onto the ship."

They all got off at the diving platform and Les asked them to go through the signals with which they'd communicate under water. "Be sure you're within sight of your assigned partner at all times," he added. "If you see something interesting and you want to swim over to investigate, take your buddy with you. Do any of you have waterproof watches?"

One member of each pair had a watch, except for Al and Freida, and Les gave them a loaner. He assigned a time when they were all to report back to the diving platform and compare notes, discuss what they'd seen, and bring up any questions they had about the identity of creatures and plants they were curious about.

Les erected a blue and white flag bearing the letter "A" on the platform. "This is to let anyone passing by, for example, in a motor boat, know that there are divers under the water, and he should steer clear of this space."

He gave them one final check on their snorkeling techniques, and made sure they had their fins buckled on securely. "You'll get all your power from your fins, and you'll have your hands free. Al, here, has an underwater camera, and he'll need his hands for taking pictures. And of course, you all need your hands for signaling."

They had all stripped down to their bathing suits, leaving their outer clothing and tote bags on the platform. "Remember to keep your fin blades parallel to the calves of your legs when moving through the water," Les said. "And just to be sure you're going to be as agile as possible in the water, I want you all to go through various strokes. Everybody off, and let's see a flutter kick, a dolphin kick, and then fin on your backs."

After they'd all shown their proficiency in these exercises, Les had them practice clearing their snorkels, and he reminded them what to do if water got into their masks or the glass became fogged.

"Water is eight hundred times heavier than air at sea level," he explained. "So when you're surrounded by water, you may feel that pressure, especially in your ears." He showed them how to equalize the pressure by pinching the ends of their noses and blowing gently.

"Everyone seems ready to dive now," he said at last. "The best way to go off is just to sit on the edge of the platform, hold your mask, and fall backward into the water. Or you can jump off in stride position." He did a countdown, and the whole group splashed into the water.

Julie gasped as she fell backward, hitting the water with her shoulder blade. Twisting frontward, she held her hands against her sides and began flutter-kicking. She felt her mouth fill with water. Uh-oh! Her snorkel was too deep. It was confusing being submerged, but she recalled Les's instructions and rose to blow out a spout of water so that she could breathe normally. She looked around, saw Al nearby and gave him the okay sign, holding her thumb and forefinger in an "O".

Then she relaxed and looked downward into the sea. The aquatic world suddenly appeared out of nowhere. Below her extended a scene of an incredible variety of shapes and colors and movements. It was like participating in a science fiction movie. Deep blue branches exploded beside a mound of bright red fingerlike extensions. Pink feathery fronds undulated beside delicate green ferny growths. A huge anemone waved searching tentacles, among which a pair of striped clownfish played.

She saw the shadow of Les finning beside her. He signaled to her and to Al to swim beyond a formation of huge plate-shaped corals in shades of yellow and pale blue, and out past a giant round coral with indentations as if fingers had been jabbed into it. Les pointed down into a gorge where the curving, scalloped lips of a giant clam some six feet wide lay in wait for passing prey. A wavering, pale light bathed the panorama as they paddled.

A couple of large blue parrot fish with giant eyes, approached to inspect Julie. They were so close she could scrutinize the beaklike mouths that gave them their name. Later, Les told her that with those beaks, the fish ground coral into sand.

They descended deeper into the water to examine a waving pink tentacle with a profusion of lime green flowers thrusting outward for nourishment, and still deeper to investigate a fluid creature composed of crimson-bordered white ruffles in constant motion. It turned out to be a nudibranch.

Julie felt water seeping into her mask. Could she remember Les's instructions? She glanced toward her buddies and gave the trouble signal, moving her hands palms down, then pointing to her mask. Les demonstrated the remedy to her by turning his body from the horizontal position, pressing the side of his mask that was uppermost, and exhaling through his nose. Julie, following his example, felt the water draining away. Another exhalation and her mask was clear. She could see her own bright air bubbles ascending through the strange, aqueous illumination of the undersea.

One visual delight followed another, and soon Al Green motioned for them to follow, while he led them toward a cave. Scores of tiny bright pink fish pulsed past them and darted into a forest of purple branch coral. Small, mushroom-like coral ovals decorated one side of the cave. Les pushed ahead of Al and Julie, warning them away, then pointing from a distance to a fantastically fringed fish that hovered near the cave mouth. The fins of the fish rayed out like a pheasant's feathers in orange, yellow and red, waving delicately, catching the pale light that filtered through the water and turning to gold and scarlet.

Les signaled with his hands that the elaborate beauty of the fish spelled danger. He glanced at his watch and pointed in the direction of the diving platform.

With fluttering fins, the trio headed for their base, picking up Wendy and Louise on the way. Les hauled himself up onto the platform, shucking his fins and tossing them aboard before he ascended. Then he helped the others up. Al and Freida were already on the platform sunning themselves. Les stood and squinted over the surface of the water until he could see Brian and Will lying face down, their flippers moving lazily, the ends of the snorkels visible. Les asked if everyone had enjoyed a good view of the reef. Louise announced that she and Wendy had encountered a large, flapping ray, and that they had taken off in fright.

"A ray isn't really that dangerous," Les said. "If he's provoked, he might give an aggressor a wicked slap with his tail, but in general he's pretty harmless, and fun to watch because his movements through the water are like poetry. In fact there's a story that someone rode on a manta ray's back once. I can't vouch for the truth of it. I'm afraid the cinema has made villains of such undersea creatures as the ray and the octopus, but neither of them deserves such a reputation. Now, the magnificent lion fish which Al just discovered flitting around the mouth of a cave is something to run from. It has venom as powerful as a snake. Watch out for cone shells, too. There's a tale that a man once picked up a beautiful cone from the reef, put it in his pocket, and was stung to death by the poisonous animal in the cone. Tonight at the lodge we can look at one of the books that will show you pictures of the poisonous creatures under the sea. We'll also see a film identifying the scores of kinds of corals we've been seeing."

Julie was mesmerized as Les poured out his knowledge of the world under the sea. His fascination and absorption with marine life was evident in the sparkle of his eyes, the lively mobility of his facial expressions and gestures as he talked. His soft Australian accent and his occasional warm glances toward her were endearing. He was undoubtedly a wonderful guy. Why did she sometimes fear his being attracted to her?

"Would you swim with Louise and me next?" Wendy asked, apparently just as fascinated as Julie was. "Al and Julie had their turn already."

"It's only fair," Julie chimed in quickly. "He shows us things we might not find—a giant clam, for instance."

"I'll agree, since Julie has a competent buddy now. I'll spread myself around."

Julie was relieved that she wouldn't be earning the group's resentment by monopolizing Les. Brian and Will had finned to the diving platform and their masked heads appeared over the edge. Brian pushed his dripping mask off reddened eyes. He and Will handed up their fins, and then scrambled onto the platform.

"My friends in Alice Springs won't believe what Brian and I saw out there," Will said. "We saw a long sea snake!"

"We'll just dry off a little," Les said. "I'll signal the launch to take us back aboard the catamaran where we'll have lunch, and after a proper interval, we'll hit the reef again."

"I'd like to see what the sub is like," Freida said. "I've decided I'm a landlubber."

"Louise and I are going to snorkel again, and don't forget, we have Les as our guide." Wendy looked pointedly at Julie.

Everyone put on shirts and coverups. The glass-bottom boat came alongside and took them aboard, depositing them at the catamaran. The group clambered on deck, ravenous for the buffet lunch that was spread on long tables on the lower deck. Big clam shells full of shrimp, salads, cold meats and cheeses, herbed chicken and pastries were arrayed there.

Julie saw Zelda enter the room, making a beeline for Les.

"Just abandoned me altogether!" she accused. "Left me stuck on the ship all morning! Once the ship stopped moving and I calmed down inside and felt like swimming, everyone was gone."

"Couldn't you have gone on the glass-bottom boat or the submarine with the other passengers?" Les asked. "I thought you'd do that."

"And get back into motion, only to get seasick again? No thank you. Why would I work so hard to pass that snorkeling test if I didn't intend to do it?"

Julie couldn't resist breaking into Zelda's tirade. "But you said you wanted to stay on the ship. I asked if you wanted to come with the others and you said you'd stay right where you were. Those were your exact words."

"I didn't mean for the whole morning. If you hadn't been in such a hurry to get back to Mr. Wonderful here, you would have found that out." She glared first at Julie and then at Les.

"Well, Miss Brentwood," Les said, attempting a soothing manner. "You can still go out after lunch. All is not lost."

"I paid for a full day, not a half day," she retorted.

Julie was outraged by the angry woman's attack. Every member of their group was listening. Al looked amused. Wendy and Louise glanced at one another with raised eyebrows. Brian took his young brother away from the argument to look over the rail.

"Come on," Freida said, wedging herself between Les and his assailant. She took Zelda's arm. "We'd better get in line or all the food will be gone before we reach the buffet." Arnold followed them, and then the others. Les gave Julie a distressed glance, but after Zelda's insinuation that Julie was distracting him from paying proper attention to the others, he didn't dare single her out as a lunch partner.

"Do they have shrimp in everything here?" Julie heard the disgruntled woman exclaim as she passed the buffet. "It doesn't agree with me. I'll break out in hives."

After lunch, they all went back to the diving platform, except for Freida and Arnold, who were going to check out the reef from the glass bottom boat and the submarine.

"You fellows doing okay?" Les asked the two brothers. "And I've seen that Julie and Al know how to handle themselves underwater." He addressed Wendy and Louise. "I'm sorry, girls, I know I promised to guide you around, but I'll have to team up with Zelda, since she has no experience. If you want to follow along with us, fine. Maybe I can lead you to some special features of the reef."

Julie was eager to stay out of Les's way, to avoid causing him further difficulties. "Come on, Al, let's submerge," she said, positioning her mask and snorkel, and strapping on her fins. They splashed backward off the platform, stroking their fins away, soaring over canyons and gorges, watching shimmering schools of tiny fish darting and turning, catching the mysterious luminescence that filtered through the sea. They passed huge jackfish and a polka-dotted barramundi cod. Al pointed downward toward a coral branch with bright red flowers. Les had told them that this type of coral was a Gorgonian. Julie held her tongue against her mouthpiece so the sea water wouldn't enter her mouth when she descended to examine a strange creature with bloated arms rayed out around a circular body, and made a mental note to ask Les about it. Al pointed to a long, spotted fish beneath them and made a gesture to surface. Ascending, Julie spouted the water from her snorkel and inhaled a big gulp of air. She turned over and finned on her back. Al followed suit.

"That was a leopard shark down there," he told Julie. "I thought we should get out of the way." Later, Les told them that the leopard shark was harmless, that it had probably looked much larger than it was. The rayed, fat creature Julie had seen was a *beche-de-mer*, or sea cucumber.

Through the afternoon, they alternately rested on the diving platform and finned over the reef, feasting their eyes on the strange shapes and riotous colors. Once, when they hoisted themselves onto the float, Zelda was lying prostrate there, breathing spasmodically. Les was daubing her reddened arm with a clear liquid.

"She tangled with a stinging coral," he explained to the others. "She ought to get some relief from this dose of vinegar."

When Zelda was able to breathe normally, Les saw her onto the glass-bottom boat, and back to the catamaran. It was almost time to return to Coral Island, and the indignant woman maligned Les all during the trip back, excoriating him for failing to warn her out of the stinging coral. "He had his mind elsewhere all the time he should have been guiding me away from danger." She glared balefully at Julie.

Back at Coral Island, Zelda reported to the reception desk that she was canceling the remainder of her stay: she had been neglected, given inadequate instruction, and placed in a perilous position by a staff member who was not concentrating on his job.

Chapter Nine

Zelda did not show up for tea that afternoon. Les seemed preoccupied, mingling among the guests with the other staff members. Neil wore an ill-tempered expression on his square-jawed face. Julie guessed that the incident with the woman from New Zealand had landed Les in hot water. Les got his snorkeling group together and spread out the book on corals and other undersea life forms. Some of the snorkelers pointed out shapes and colors they had viewed through their masks that afternoon. Les showed them a fringed starfish.

"We'll see these tomorrow," he told them. "This is one of the most destructive creatures on the reef. It isn't dangerous to humans, but it's a threat to the living coral." Les described the behavior of this unusual starfish, called the Crown of Thorns. It would drape itself over a head of coral and completely consume all of the live polyps, leaving dead coral behind. "The life of the reef is based on coral building up on itself, and so the biologists are concerned about this unpleasant animal, which spreads over the reef like weeds. A bounty has been offered in the past to divers and snorkelers for each one of these animals brought in."

Now and then Les cast a desperate glance at Julie. They had not been together since the morning, and Julie could see that something was bugging Les. He went back with the other staff members after tea without addressing a word to Julie individually.

When Julie went to dinner, she saw Zelda sitting at a table alone and went to speak to her. "I'm sorry about your injury," she said. "I hope it's better now."

"It's a little late for you to be concerned, after monopolizing and distracting our leader so that he wasn't giving our group the proper supervision," Zelda said snappishly. The hostility on the woman's face made it obvious that she didn't welcome Julie's sympathy or her company. An angry retort formed in Julie's mind. Zelda should be told that such an incompetent swimmer as herself shouldn't have attempted diving, that she had hampered Les's leadership of the group and dampened their enjoyment of the day on the reef. But Julie held her angry words in. They could only anger Zelda further. An older person wouldn't take seriously what a teenager had to say anyway.

After her gesture of friendship had been rebuffed, Julie could only turn and walk back to the table where the rest of the snorkeling group had assembled.

"The old battle-axe put you in your place, Julie?" Al asked. He had been observing the interchange.

"I only stopped to tell her I hoped she was feeling better. I felt sorry for her, sitting over there alone."

"I expect she's accustomed to being alone. She makes a career of antagonizing people," Louise said.

"I was in the office when she was complaining about Les," Brian said. "I think she got him in trouble with the management."

"It's a shame. He does a fine job," Al said.

"She claimed he wasn't giving the other members of the group enough attention, and he was too absorbed in Julie," Brian said. "Of course, I can't say I blame him." He gave Julie a mischievous smile, and Julie felt conspicuous and embarrassed.

"We got enough attention," Freida said. "Arnold and I got the basics from him, and then we just wanted to explore on our own."

"Sure. Who wants a nursemaid hovering around?" Arnold agreed.

"Will and I were doing fine, too, having fun," Brian said.

"Maybe Louise and I were asking for more of his time," Wendy said. "But we just thought he could show us some special fish and coral that we wouldn't find on our own."

"As for any other interest in him, he's a little young for us, after all. What is he? Eighteen, nineteen? Even if we had been bitten or stung down there, we never would have complained to the management," Louise added. "That was purely spiteful. He was a good snorkeling instructor, and he knows everything about the reef."

"Maybe we should neutralize that witch's complaints by giving him a commendation," Al suggested.

"I'm game," Arnold agreed. They decided to write a letter signed by the whole group, expressing their appreciation for Les. Julie signed it eagerly, for she felt to blame for his problems.

After dinner, they went to the film on undersea life. Another staff member ran the projector, and Julie was conscious of Les slipping into the seat beside her. He shouldn't be there. If his interest in her was causing talk and trouble for him around the island, he shouldn't be flaunting it.

She brought the subject up after the movie, when they were walking back to her cabin. "I'm afraid my being here is jeopardizing your job," she said. "Your boss, Neil, has commented twice about it, and I heard that Zelda made some complaint today that might have caused you some difficulty."

"It was my bad luck to get that chronic malcontent in my group. It's my own fault for accepting her. I should have told her yesterday she didn't have the skills to snorkel and that I couldn't take the responsibility for her. Instead, I tried to work along with her and the whole thing boomeranged on me. I was dressed down by Neil in front of the whole staff. Sure, everyone has noticed I can't keep my mind or my eyes off you. It's true. I told you yesterday I've fallen in love with you, Julie. If you loved me back, you'd know that it's total commitment and nothing can be done about it."

"Les, you're not being sensible. I'm only in this country for a short time. We shouldn't fall in love. We live on different continents! We'll never see one another after I leave next week."

"Don't remind me of that. And don't ask me to be sensible. You have a mysterious attraction for me that can't be analyzed by any logic, so don't try to make sense of it. Besides, we will see each other again. I may follow you back to America."

Les was holding Julie's hand, and she couldn't pull it away. Yet she didn't want Les to love her that much. It was scary, now that he was convincing her he was serious. She didn't know what to do about it, especially when he pulled her close and kissed her, sending all her logical thoughts flying out among the palm fronds that were silhouetted against the night sky.

"You do love me, Julie, I can feel it," he insisted. "We were meant for each other. Did you ever hear of Kismet—that's an ancient word from Persia or somewhere around there. It means fate. You were fated to come here with your father so we could meet. It's written in the stars!" They looked up at the stars which were brilliant above the island, and just as Julie found the Southern Cross again, Les blotted it out with another kiss.

Julie feared she was falling under his spell. He was making her as giddy as he was. She needed to get away from him and think of more reasons why she shouldn't fall for him. When he was so near, there were too many impulses pulling her in the other direction.

Julie wished she could tell Les it was past her curfew, that her parents would be waiting up for her. She longed for her dad, remembering their conversation in the hotel room. She was accumulating more things she'd like to talk over with him. Would she have the nerve to ask her dignified dad to explain a guy's feelings to her, so she'd be more in control? Right now, she wasn't too responsible. The impossibly romantic scent of tropical flowers and the sound of gently lapping water lulled a person into thinking there was no tomorrow, that time and the universe were all encapsulated in this one magic moment.

She had never experienced such a feeling when she'd been with Mike. Her attachment to her old boyfriend seemed trivial and childish.

"I think I'd better get back to my cabin," Julie said. She needed to separate herself from Les to sort out her tumultuous feelings.

"So early?" Les objected. Julie took his hand from the clasp of his.

"Oh, by the way," she said. "I never got a chance to tell you I talked to Dad this morning and he's coming out on

Friday evening by motorboat, and bringing your sister and her boyfriend out. They'll stay over until Sunday and then I'll go back with them."

"Jane and Richard coming out!" Les exclaimed. "That is a surprise! Jane was determined I shouldn't have all the time with you! Now we'll have only two more days alone. Alone! We don't even have that. I have all those snorkelers! Julie, it's such torment to have to snatch a moment now and then with you while I'm working."

"I've been concerned about that, Les," Julie said. "It's obvious that my being here is distracting you from your job. You'll be much better off when I leave. Anyway, this whole attachment of yours is insane. You have got to cool it. All we can be is friends. There will be a whole ocean between us in a few days."

"Don't talk about going. I don't want to think of a time when you're gone."

They had reached the steps of Cabin 5, and Les said, "We can't end the evening this early, when it's my only chance to talk to you. Let me come in with you for a while."

Julie became superalert at that suggestion. A sudden doubt swept over her about Les. She wondered if he'd said the same words to other girls who had visited the island. She thought about her dad, and of his confidence that she could handle independence. The image of her brother, Harlan, flitted through her thoughts. Harlan had always been a fiercely independent person, an activist who always did what seemed right to him, even though kids around school had sometimes ridiculed him for it.

Independence must run in the family. Her dad wandered around the world investigating matters on his own, and couldn't be confined in a stuffy office. Her mother also had her own job and wasn't dependent upon anyone. That was the way the Blackers were, and Julie was one of them. Basically, she thought Les was crazy for falling in love with her—if he really had—and she wasn't going to multiply his folly by letting the same thing happen to her.

"No, you can't come in, Les. But we can sit on the porch for a few minutes. I'll make you a hot chocolate for the road."

All of the hotel rooms in Australia seemed to have tea kettles, with instant coffee and tea, and on Coral Island, there were also some little packets of chocolate. Julie turned on the switch and poured hot water over the chocolate powder. She heard Les open the door and come in. "Here, you can carry yours out," she said, shooing him out the door with the aromatic cup of chocolate. Her mother would disapprove of a guy being in her room, especially way out here on Coral Island, where she was on her own. She closed the door firmly behind her and set her chocolate on the small table on the little veranda that faced the forest. The perfumed air mingled with the scent of cocoa.

"I know so little about you, Les. Why don't you tell me your life story?"

"You know everything about me," Les protested. "You've been in my house, met my family, seen me doing my job. What else is there to know?"

"But there's more than that. I want to know what it was like for you growing up. How did you get interested in being a marine biologist? And maybe you think I'm nosy, but I'd like to know about your friends back home, especially your girlfriends."

"Checking up on me? I get a feeling that you don't quite trust me, Julie, but if my life history is what you want, then prepare to be bored for a few hours." Julie saw Les relax and his intensity diminish as he delved back into his childhood and recounted pranks he and Jane had played on one another, stories about adventures he and a boyhood chum had experienced roaming the Queensland rain forests. "The forests were larger then," he recalled. "We used to climb up the vines that wind around the tall trees and find birds' nests and tree kangaroos and possums sleeping. When we became older and a lot of the forests were being logged, my friend and I joined a movement to stop it. We used to lie across the road in front of the logging trucks to protest. But it didn't do much good. Even my own father has cleared out lots of land that used to be forest, for his cane fields."

"You remind me of my brother, Harlan, who's always trying to save the environment. You and he would get along great."

"I hope to meet him some day. I intend to follow you, Julie."

"Don't start that again, Les. You still haven't told me about your interest in the sea, or about your girlfriends."

Les went on to tell about childhood visits to the beaches and offshore islands along the coast, where he learned to snorkel and scuba dive, developing his intense interest in marine life. "When I got the job out here for the vacation months, it was such a major goal of mine that I didn't want to leave it to go to college, as I told you. I had a first-class row with Father over it, and we compromised. I've promised to quit after this year and go to college."

"You meet a lot of girls out here," Julie pursued. "You probably have had numerous girlfriends."

"Here today and gone tomorrow," Les said, shrugging. "Certainly part of our job is to entertain guests, and I and the other staff members have shown some of these young ladies some fun on the island, but every girl I've ever known faded out of my memory when I met you."

"If you're supposed to entertain guests, why does Neil object to your paying attention to me?"

"He can plainly see it's not a casual thing, that it's real. You do distract me from my job, and Neil has seen that. Now, turnabout is fair play. You have to reveal all about your boyfriends back in California."

"That's a very short story," Julie said. She told Les about Mike and how he'd gone off to college and hadn't come back.

"So now you're wary about trusting people?" Les asked.

They heard Freida and Arnold opening the door in front of the cabin, the lights were turned on and the couple came out onto the back porch, greeting Les and Julie.

"We saw the flying foxes," Freida exclaimed. "There were dozens of them. What are you having? Chocolate. A good idea. Arnold and I will join you."

Arnold questioned Les about the next day's activities, and learned that they'd snorkel on another lavishly vegetated part of the reef. He described some of the creatures they were likely to see.

Julie felt a yawn surfacing and decided to excuse herself, pleading the always useful jet lag.

"I'm boring you with my marine life descriptions," Les said in a clownishly injured tone.

"Of course not, only I'm afraid I'll have to see those sights tomorrow rather than hear about them tonight. If I don't get some sleep I'll just see little blurs going past my mask."

"We all should retire," Arnold agreed. "After all, Freida and I are farm people, up with the birds."

"I'll come by as soon as I can tomorrow morning," Les said. Despite the fact that Freida and Arnold were nearby, still finishing their chocolate, Les gave Julie a lingering goodnight kiss. "Sleep well, little mermaid," he said. Arnold and Freida looked the other way.

Everyone on the island seemed to know about Les's pursuit of Julie. For instance, one of the girls who came in to change the linens remarked, scrutinizing Julie, "You're Les Donaldson's sweetheart, aren't you?"

One of Les's fellow snorkeling instructors said with a grin the next day when they were viewing another part of the reef, "You sure have Donaldson in a spin."

These comments were accumulating to convince Julie that Les was sincere, that he wasn't just putting on an act. If Les had lived in Blossom Valley and had fallen for her, she would have been thrilled. But over here, on this short vacation in Australia, his attention made her feel strange and a little fearful. She determined not to let herself flip over him. She would just be heading for heartbreak city. Julie promised herself to control it, keep it light and casual, a time they could both enjoy remembering.

So the next day, out on the reef, Julie suggested that they pair up with a variety of different buddies, while Les circulated among the various pairs showing them interesting aspects of the area. Julie finned with Brian, while his younger brother became the partner of Louise, and Wendy and Al were buddies. She learned that Wendy and Louise had come from Perth, way out in Western Australia, that Louise was a musician, playing in a chamber orchestra, that Will and Brian had been orphans since Brian was fourteen, and that Brian had practically raised and supported Will.

Les went from pair to pair pointing out the damsel fish that lived in the protection of the branches of staghorn coral, and the small gobies, which, chameleon-like, changed colors to match the coral in which they hid.

He pointed out the trumpetfish, which rides on the back of other fish to stalk its prey. Under Les's guidance, they saw the interdependence between a shrimp and a goby. The shrimp, which has poor eyesight, dug a burrow while the goby watched and flicked its tail to warn the shrimp of predators. Then the shrimp and the goby shared the burrow. He pointed out to all of his group the wrasses which flutter and jerk about larger fish, cleaning them of parasites and dead skin.

At the end of the day, the whole group was enthusiastic about the mixing up of pairs, which had led them to become more knowledgeable and better acquainted with one another. The film that evening was on sea birds, and the program for the next day was to go to Noddy Cay, where they would see the great profusion of sea birds and be able to snorkel as well. Les told them to bring their sun-tan oil and dark glasses, for the sugary sand created an intense glare.

On the approach to the cay the next day, Julie could see that it was even smaller than Coral Island. There was a wide strip of dazzling white sand, and in the center a mound of low vegetation appeared, but there were no trees. The ship anchored and the group was brought to land on the launch. A huge congregation of black birds was identified by Les as noddy terns. "They're very tame, and the vegetated area of the cay is their nesting ground. We're not supposed to go beyond the line where the sand ends, because this is a bird sanctuary."

Wendy and Louise said they weren't going to snorkel. They wanted to lie in the sand to improve their suntans. Al had brought a camera with a zoom lens, and he was engrossed in taking closeups of the birds in various postures.

"I've never seen so many birds all in one place!" Julie exclaimed as a great cloud of white birds rustled suddenly into the sky, wheeling and soaring, and as suddenly settled back to earth.

"Those are crested terns." Les led Freida and Arnold, Will and Brian and Julie down the shore where they could look closely at these birds, which had a shock of unruly-looking black feathers on top of their heads, looking like punk hairdos. The cay was so small they could walk the whole length of the beach in ten minutes, even stopping to see a white-fronted sooty tern feeding her speckled chick.

"These birds aren't afraid of us at all!" Will exclaimed in delight. "I can even go close to the nests where the mother birds are sitting on their eggs."

"Don't go too close." Les pointed to a low, scrubby vegetation in the middle of the island. "The birds look tamer than they are. If you should walk near a nest and frighten the mother bird away, one of those watchful gulls could move right in and destroy the eggs, or kill any small chicks."

Arnold and Freida stopped to take pictures of each other. Les told what was left of the group that the snorkeling wasn't as good here as it had been on the reefs they'd explored before. "There's a lot of dead coral on the fringe around the Cay," he said, "thanks to the Crown of Thorns starfish which I told you about last night. We'll swim out and see if we can find some of those animals."

Les and Julie, Brian and Will waded out in their snorkeling equipment and finned into deeper water. At first they saw only desolate, colorless canyons of dead coral, where a few fish darted. Moving on, they encountered formations of varicolored live plate coral. Descending to a cavern, they confronted the hostile visage of a moray eel, and they quickly sped away. Then they found a colony of Crown of Thorns, with their radiating, fringed clinging arms. Les pulled a couple of them off the devastated coral.

Will signaled that he was tired, and they made the return journey to the cay.

All of the group rested in the sand after they had examined the destructive starfish. Les took Julie away from the others, to the opposite end of the island. "We need some time together, Julie," he said. "All of my group is settled down, being lazy. Now's our chance. Do you realize that this is Thursday already? We only have another day left."

"But I'm not leaving until Sunday afternoon."

"The weekend doesn't count. Remember, we're going to be invaded tomorrow by your dad and Jane and Richard. We'll have no privacy, and I have so many private things to say to you before you leave. Julie, we weren't meant to meet and then part and forget about each other. You're the love of my life. There's never going to be anyone I feel this way about. What are we going to do about it, Julie? Last night I stayed awake, wondering how I could endure having you go away, and I knew I couldn't. The way I love you, it's like Romeo and Juliet, Lancelot and Guinevere, and it's not going to go away. Don't try to brush it off as a vacation romance, Julie, because I'm serious, and it's forever."

Chapter Ten

Julie was reclining in the warm sand, and Les had propped himself up on his elbow, his mesmerized gaze exploring her face. A powerful feeling for him washed through her, but she wasn't going to let herself love him.

"You're a terrific, impressive guy, Les," she said, sitting up and looking squarely at him. "I'm flattered that you have these feelings for me, but I don't really want you to love me. You're fooling yourself to think it's forever, because after this weekend we won't see one another again, and I'll be halfway across the world a few days after that. You're only going to make yourself miserable if you let yourself think you're in love."

"There's no question of 'letting myself,'" Les said. "It just happened. It's real. I'm not just thinking it. You've seen those comical pictures of Cupid shooting an arrow into someone's heart? I know how that legend originated, because I could almost feel that shaft going through me when you walked out that airport door. I haven't been the same since. A feeling like that isn't something a person can control. I have to find a way of assuring that even though you go, we can look forward to being together again—to know that I'll be in your memory until we do meet again."

"Les, of course you're going to stay in my memory. How could I ever forget you? I've never known a guy like you. We could write to one another, but I'm afraid that when people are apart, they soon develop other interests and one forgets about the other. I've been through it, and so I know it's useless to make any commitments or promises."

Even though Les was older than Julie, she felt more mature just now than he was. He was absolutely unreasonable, ruled by his emotions. "I'm not even through high school, Les. I'm only sixteen. I'm not ready to talk about forever. We shouldn't be sitting here holding such a heavy conversation. Let's get our minds off this useless nonsense. I don't have much more time to explore the reef, which is what I came out here to do."

Julie picked up her snorkel and stuck her mask on top of her head. She shooed Les out of the sand with one of her flippers and his expression of romantic melancholy changed to one of teasing vengeance.

"Useless nonsense is it?" He chased her down the sand. Julie sat in the edge of the water slipping her flipper straps up over her heels and then she splashed backward until she hit deep water. She pulled down her mask, inserted her snorkel and pushed herself to finning position. It was a windless day. Her view through the water was unmarred by wave-stirred debris. She could see a long distance. Propelling herself rapidly across the sandy fringe around the island, she hit coral. There was no color here, and few fish to be seen. This was a desert of dead coral being eroded into sand by the tides.

Les moved up beside her, pointing to the left, and she turned with him, their bodies moving in unison. Once she felt his hand touch hers and she turned and their eyes met behind the masks. Gliding on, they saw the plateau of coral skeletons fall off into a canyon whose walls were formed of coral stretching out into elongated flanges of a myriad of textures. The sunlight filtered through the water, illuminating glistening coral flowers of gold, orange and pink.

Skirting the coral-lined canyon wall, Les led Julie to a shallow valley where brightly colored fish sucked up sand and sifted it in clouds through their gills. Julie and Les surfaced, exhaling water from their tubes like a couple of fountains.

Julie had learned to be at home in the undersea world. The equipment became part of her. The weird shapes and variety of patterns of the fish, the delicacy of the coral polyps, had taken on such a fascination for her that she could snorkel for long periods of time without getting tired or bored.

It was ebb tide. Julie and Les reached a shelf of coral which was being exposed by the receding ocean. They stood watching a flight of terns hover-feeding in the shallow water. They saw a waterfall develop when the tide exposed a canyon wall. Tide pools remained where the sea retreated from the coral plateau. Les and Julie peered into their teeming depths, where anemones waved with small clownfish dancing among their tentacles and hermit crabs pranced comically about in hand-me-down shells. Exquisite tiny fish remained trapped in the pools. From his seemingly infinite store of knowledge about sea life, Les explained in his soft, flowing foreign voice many of the secrets of the tidepools. Then they dived into the canyon beyond the plateau. A profusion of coral shapes emerged from its walls. A school of fat pink fish swam around and beneath the two snorkel-

ers. A large grouper, its lower jar protruding from its ugly
face, approached and sent the pink fish scurrying off into a
forest of blue staghorn coral.

Time passed in a haze of wonder for Julie in this dream
world under the sea until Les gave her a signal to turn back
and they finned in the direction of the cay. Julie could feel
Les's eyes fixed on her through the mask. He slithered in
close to her and held her hand as they neared the cay. They
were still holding hands when they emerged from the sea.
They removed their fins and proceeded up the burning sand.
Julie was exhilarated by her hour among the creatures of the
sea. She shook out her dripping hair, inhaled the briny air,
and listened to the myriad calls of the sea birds that congre-
gated on the sand and wheeled over the cay.

"It's about time you turned up, Donaldson." The exasperated voice of Kevin broke into Julie's idyllic reverie. Les
turned with a dream-like smile toward his fellow worker,
who had come over on the catamaran with them to super-
vise a second group of visitors from Coral Island.

"The time passes before you know it on a day like this,"
Les said.

"You better be conscious of the time, Donaldson," the
usually amiable Kevin said, scowling. "Some of your un-
supervised people have been getting in trouble out here with
the rangers. Roaming all over the place where they shouldn't
be. I've gotten stuck with some of your group when I already have too many people of my own to manage. What's
going on with you, Donaldson—as if I couldn't guess."
Kevin gave Julie a calculating glance. "You're headed for
trouble, Donaldson, if you don't start putting business before pleasure."

Julie's euphoric mood crashed into distress. She was
nothing but bad news for Les.

"What happened?" Les asked, looking concerned.

"Those two girls, Wendy somebody and her friend, went around on the forbidden side of the island. Then this chap, the younger brother of one of your group, was trespassing on the nesting grounds and picked up a baby tern. Brought it down to show to his brother just as the rangers came ashore for their inspection. They read the riot act. Said if the Coral Island staff couldn't keep their visitors in line, they'd be banned from the Cay in the future. I tried to calm them down, but you know how rigid rangers are. They're not willing to bend at all, when it comes to their regulations. I hope they don't make a formal complaint to the Coral Island management, which, as you know, is quite sternly regimented itself. You know the particular person to whom I refer."

"I never imagined they'd go off the beach. I made the usual announcement that they weren't to venture into the vegetated portion of the island. I thought they were all settled down sun-bathing, and they wouldn't need me for a while. Al was going to photograph birds, the girls and Arnold and Freida looked as if they were napping in the sand, and Will and Brian never cause trouble. It seemed to be a good time to show Julie some sights."

"It turned out to be an inopportune time, since your people didn't stay where they were put. Anyway, Donaldson, I have my hands full with a group of newcomers, and I'll appreciate your looking after those who were assigned to you."

There wasn't much of the day left. During the time they remained on the cay, Les routed the rest of his charges out of the sand and walked them back and forth across the island, identifying the various birds until they could tell four types of terns apart and could identify the fierce black frigate bird which followed the brown booby birds on their fishing expeditions and stole their fish from them as they returned.

Then he took the rest of the group snorkeling. Julie said she had had enough and she sat in the sand brooding over Les's destructive attachment for her. He was even losing Kevin's friendship. Would Kevin's scolding make him see the light? Maybe he would discontinue his pursuit of Julie.

Even though Julie had urged Les to cool it, she wasn't sure she wanted him to. His ardent attention was exciting. Part of her wanted to find out what it would lead to. He was getting to her. There was no doubt he was a terrific guy: intelligent, good-looking, amiable and capable. His overemotional nature and impracticality might be faults, but they were endearing ones. Julie couldn't criticize him for neglecting his job when she was the cause of it. He had convinced her by now that he was sincere. He really did love her, or at least thought he did. When she left, he'd get over it. Julie couldn't quite figure why he had gone so overboard, unless it was, that being foreign, she was a novelty. Guys back at her high school in the United States didn't fall all over themselves about her. She was just an ordinary person in Blossom Valley. She did okay in school, but she wasn't counted among the school's brains. Her looks were average, too. No one had ever accused her of being a beauty, but Les, with his distorted view of her, might. She wasn't a big shot at school, like a student body officer. So why was Les so impressed with her? He must see something about her that nobody else could see. Anyway, he could make her feel special, important and attractive.

When the catamaran deposited the passengers from the cay back on Coral Island, Les said to Julie, "I'll see you at tea." He was busy collecting the snorkeling gear. Julie rushed to her cabin to shower off the sand and sea water.

But Les was not at tea when Julie, her hair freshly washed and drying in feathery tendrils around her face, appeared in the lounge dressed in her aquamarine shift with the big pink and gold fish handpainted on the front. She kept watching the door for him. Most of the other staff members were there. Julie talked for a while to Rana, the botanist, who told her how birds had planted seeds to start the scanty vegetation on Noddy Cay, where they had spent the day.

Julie didn't want to ask the other staff members where Les was, reminding them of the bond that had developed between her and Les during the week. She felt lonely in his absence, and wandered from the lounge to the terrace to watch the sunset over the sea through a tangle of pandanus palms. On the rocks below the ledge, the mottled brown and beige whimbrels clustered, and Julie heard the soft call of a fruit dove. The aroma of food being prepared in the lodge kitchen mingled with the fresh scent of the sea and the perfume of flowering tropical trees.

Coral Island was a dream world, unreal and impermanent in Julie's life. Les's professed love would be just as evanescent. She must have brought so much trouble that he'd decided to drop her. She longed to see him, to find out what was the matter.

Les still had not appeared at dinner time. Julie sat at the table with the usual crowd.

"It's the last evening for us," Wendy said. "Louise and I will be leaving on the eleven o'clock ship tomorrow."

"Freida and I will be joining you," Arnold said. "We're going on south for a few days on the Capricorn Islands, down at the end of the reef, and then home."

"We're staying till Sunday," Brian said. "Then Will has to get back. He's missing school."

Al Green was staying on until Sunday, too.

"You'll get to meet my dad, who's arriving tomorrow," Julie said. "Along with Les's sister and her boyfriend."

"Where is Les, anyway?" Al asked. "I didn't see him at tea."

"I was wondering the same thing," Julie said.

Les finally appeared at the after dinner film, for he was the operator of it this evening. He greeted them in a rather formal manner, announcing that the audience would learn about the various types of fish inhabiting the reef. During the showing, Julie frequently took her eyes from the screen to look toward Les, and he always happened to be looking at her at the same time. When their glances met, something like an electric shock would go through her. There was a disturbing current. Apprehension mixed with affection churned inside her. She couldn't concentrate on the movie. She wasn't really listening to the commentary, and the fish were all mixed up like a kaleidoscope.

Near the end of the film, Les sat briefly in an empty chair next to hers. "I have to return the film to staff headquarters," he whispered. "Afterward, we'll get together." He was out of the chair and back to his projector before Julie could answer.

What was she supposed to do? Where did he expect to meet her? The film ended, and Les, in a poised announcement that masked any difficulties he might be having, told the audience that he hoped they'd enjoyed the film and were having a pleasant stay on Coral Island. Then he and another guy ran the film back on its reel, put it in a can and folded up the screen and the tripod on which the projector was mounted. Les got a grip on all the equipment and set out for staff headquarters with it, while the other guy folded and stacked the chairs.

The audience drifted away, and the lights in the arcade where they'd shown the films went out. Julie wandered to the lodge patio, where the chairs had been placed up on the tables. It was spooky around the island when everyone had gone in. Besides, Julie was sleepy. The strenuous swim with Les and the day in the sea air exhausted her energy. She felt a moment of exasperation with Les for making such a vague and mysterious date with her. She was not going to meet him. He could just wait until tomorrow for whatever it was he had to tell her.

She walked through the balmy, perfumed darkness, the ghostly white shapes of herons appearing above her in the dense forest canopy, and let herself into her cabin. She had left her salty bathing suit on the towel rod, and she had just started to rinse it out when she heard a cautious knock on the door. Her heart jumped into her throat.

"Who's there?" she asked, as though she didn't know.

"It's Les. Let me in."

Julie opened the door a crack, her heart still pounding crazily. "Wait a minute, Les. I'll come out. I don't allow guys in my room."

Julie slipped out the door, and Les seized her, pressing her against him, his hands seeming to be everywhere. "I thought I'd never get away." He was panting as if he'd been running. "Neil has got me on probation. He's piling all these extra jobs on me."

"Sit down, Les. Cool off." Julie wriggled from his embrace. She had heard in various gossip sessions with her girlfriends that guys have a lot less self-control than girls, so that left the responsibility to set limits to her.

"I don't want to sit across the table from you. Let's at least sit on the steps, where you'll be close to me."

"Not too close, Les. You're scaring me. Don't be so intense."

"Sorry, Julie. I came over here at top speed. I've been so eager to be with you that I hardly know what I'm doing."

Les seemed very excited. She mustn't let him get out of hand on this last night she'd be alone on the island. Tomorrow her dad and Les's sister would be here. Even though he was overwrought and emotional, Julie felt such sympathy for him that she couldn't draw away when he calmed down and encircled her in his arm and told her his troubles.

"First, you remember, Zelda complained that I'd been neglecting her and she canceled her reservation. That was number one check against me, unless you count that minor episode when you and that chap from Melbourne blundered into the staff sanctuary."

"I'm sorry, Les. I've caused you nothing but trouble."

"It's worth anything I have to endure to know you, Julie. If I may repeat myself, you're the love of my life."

"Les, you're exaggerating. I'm just a passing episode."

"I'll never let you be that, Julie."

"I don't deserve all your attention."

Les tightened his arm around her and kissed her forehead.

"Neil has accumulated all sorts of minor complaints against me. One night I had Kevin bring back the film equipment when it was my turn. Kevin was going back, anyway. What difference did it make?"

"He's unfair. He's picking on you, I can see. Both he and Zelda are sourpusses with no sense of humor."

"I know. It's just my bad luck to be supervised by such a martinet as Neil."

"It will be a good thing for you when I leave the island, Les. You shouldn't have let me interfere with your work. It's not worth it for the short time you'll know me."

"Don't talk like that, Julie. I'm going to know you forever. Wait and see."

"What an impossible dream, when we live halfway around the world from each other." Julie wanted to tell him that she wished his dreams could come true, but she restrained herself. If she gave Les any indication that she returned his feelings, he might get on such a high that he'd get out of control.

"Anyway, Julie, I had a difficult time getting this job in the first place. I had to pound and pound away at them. Most of the staff people are older than I am—they've been to university. Kevin had been to Canada to get a scuba instructing certificate. I made such a nuisance of myself that they finally hired me for a summer job, and then I persuaded them again to let me stay on through the rest of the year."

"I know how persistent you can be."

"You might find out more about that," Les predicted, and Julie felt an apprehensive constriction inside.

"Today was the coup de grace for me, when those galahs trespassed around the cay."

"Galahs?"

"Those are stupid pink birds like parrots that wander helter-skelter around the farmers' fields making pests of themselves. We call senseless people galahs. Apparently, these girls, Wendy and Louise, couldn't read the signs that said Don't Walk Beyond This Point. And Will wasn't listening when I told him the birds were not to be disturbed. The Coral Island management takes it very seriously when we get a citation from the rangers, and Neil puts all the blame for these things on me. He says I'm in peril of being discharged."

"You should never have invited me here."

"Don't blame yourself, Julie. I can't think of what I was living for before I met you. Now we arrive at what I really came to tell you. I have a scheme. Tomorrow is our last day to be together before our families descend upon us and consume all our time. Friday is a slow day, and I've always had the afternoon free. Most of the group will be leaving.

Freida and Arnold, Wendy and Louise. Those remaining can go on the botanical tour with Rana, or out in the glass-bottom boat. You and I are going to spend the whole afternoon together exploring the reef. I'm going to show you things nobody gets to see, places I've explored on my time off, which I want to share with you."

"You have me in suspense."

"It will be an afternoon you'll always remember."

"I already have some permanent memories. Like today, when we were at the edge of the reef. I can still hear the roar of the water running down the coral shelf into the sea."

"That was one of the places where you feel the grand structure of the reef."

Julie cuddled into the curve of Les's arm and they were silent a moment, remembering the beauty of their hours together under the sea.

"Of all the people I've ever gone finning with, you're my favorite mate," Les said.

"I love to go with you. You know so much," Julie said. "You're sure it's okay for us to go? It won't land you in more trouble?"

"You're not to worry. Just to enjoy."

Julie spent the next morning waiting for Les, wandering around the island, thinking of what she'd show her dad when he arrived. She went to the pier and saw Wendy and Louise, Arnold and Freida off. On Sunday, she'd be pulling off and leaving Les standing on the pier. It was something she didn't like to think about. Les was becoming important to her.

At noon, Julie waited in the patio, as she had arranged with Les. His eyes gleamed with anticipation and he radiated energy as he scurried to buy Julie a sandwich for lunch. Julie wore some tennis shoes and old cut-off jeans with her bathing suit underneath, and Les wore trunks with his Coral Island T-shirt. He carried their snorkeling gear in a string bag. They set off through the forest, pushing aside vines, walking over crunchy twigs and leaves, frightening a pair of pastel-colored doves from the ground into the crown of pandanus palm.

"We're off the trail," Julie said.

"I know. This is a secret mission. I don't want to encounter anyone. Today is just for you and me."

When they passed out of the forest and onto the beach, they were at the opposite side of the island, and there were no sunbathers. A few bleached logs lay on the beach, and the dessicated, broken trunks of some ancient trees jutted from the sand. Les headed for a hidden inlet surrounded by scrubby brush.

"Just a few of the staff people use this boat on their free time, to fish or explore," Les explained, helping Julie in. He untied the small, weathered craft from a stump to which it was attached, and pushed off with an oar, guiding the boat from the inlet out into the sea, where he stroked at the rope that activated the outboard motor. He tossed Julie a visor from his equipment bag. "The sun is pretty intense today," he said. Les looked relaxed, carefree. The worries of the day before had dropped away, and they were off on their own.

Les guided the flimsy craft over the placid sea to a location where the reef was partially exposed. They leaped out, drawing the boat to a sandy stretch so that it couldn't be washed away. The pair waded along through the shallow water, and crouched where tidepools appeared, then donned their snorkeling equipment and finned in the deeper water about the edge of the reef, letting parrot fish nibble their fingers, examining the strange shapes of coral that embellished the edges of deep pools. The bright blue flash of a giant clam appeared between the edges of its scalloped shell. Les and Julie glided and fluttered rhythmically together in the undersea world as if they were marine creatures themselves.

Chapter Eleven

They pulled the boat from its mooring and floated through the sea. "Now we're arriving at the main feature of the day," Les said. "There are hundreds of wrecks around the reef, many of them sunk under so much water that you need to carry an air cylinder and dive deep to see them. This one is partly exposed. You wouldn't really be aware of the total character of the reef without seeing at least one wreck." He propelled the boat through the water until it sputtered into view of an old hulk of a ship, partially exposed in front, its stern sunk in the sea.

"Is this it?" Julie exclaimed excitedly.

"It's our destination." Les smiled with satisfaction. He guided the boat to the side of the wreck and tied it to a metal cable that bulged from a jagged hole in the side of the old cargo ship. He then grabbed the cable and hoisted himself up the side of the vessel, holding his hand to support Julie as she made her way up, climbing over jagged, rusty metal to the ruined deck of the old craft. He slung his bag of snorkeling equipment down.

Their feet made hollow metallic sounds as they walked over the deck, and then skirted around a trap door from which a corroded old fire hose spilled. A portion of the rail had been eaten away by time and weather. A pair of silver gulls perched on what was left of it.

"No one can estimate how many ships have sunk up and down the length of the reef," Les told her. "They've accumulated over many years—sailing ships of past centuries, whaling ships, huge World War II transports sunk by German U-boats, the U-boats themselves, all of them and many more have ended their journeys here. This is one of the few in this area you can see without breathing apparatus."

"You've been here before."

"Some of us came out here a couple of months ago on our afternoon off. One of the staff members has done a lot of salvage diving, and he's always looking for wrecks. This one, of course, is pretty well picked over."

"Were you looking for sunken treasure?" Julie asked, her eyes sparkling with visions of brass-banded casks spilling out a fortune in emeralds, diamonds, rubies and pearls, or a pirate's hoard of ancient Spanish coins.

"Salvage divers always hope to run across something of fabulous value, of course," Les said. "Most wrecks yield only scrap metal, artifacts, old cannons and the like. You take this wreck." Les led her into the remnants of the bridge, from which the captain had steered the ship. "There were instruments here, and lots of brass. All of those items have been pried off, even the steering wheel. Maybe the owners of the ship removed them, maybe scavengers."

"I wonder if anyone was killed in the shipwreck?"

"They had a pretty good chance of surviving," Les said, "since the whole ship wasn't submerged."

"They might have been blown here by a storm."

"Or it could have been that the captain didn't have an accurate map of the reef."

"They suddenly crashed against it and it tore the ship open. The guys from the sunken part could have rushed up here, and they didn't necessarily drown."

Les and Julie walked along the slanting deck. "Here," Les said, "might have been a part of the rail where the life boats hung. The crew might have rowed to land."

"Let's hope so," Julie said.

They ran across some long pipes and hoists which Les said indicated this was a small cargo ship. "There's a lot more of the ship underwater," Les said. "We'll have to swim below to see the rest." He headed for the snorkels, masks and fins, and they turned toward the portion of the old wreck that slanted into the sea. Julie spit into her mask to keep it from fogging, rinsed it out in sea water, and then strapped it over her mouth and nose, with her snorkel in place. Les helped her on with her fins, and when his equipment was in place, they tipped backward off the rusty deck into the water which lapped against the old hulk.

Julie felt the weight of her body lighten, the effortless thrust of the water beneath her holding her up, decreasing the burden of gravity. They finned along the metal side of the wreck until a gap appeared, and they glided in under the deck on which they had just been walking. Sea water extended three-quarters of the way up the walls, so that their snorkels still extended into air, but it was stale air, rusty and cloying, and the upper deck cut off sunlight.

The dark water only vaguely revealed a passageway, at the end of which a metal doorway yawned. Finning down the passage, they noticed that the door had rusted off its hinges, and its outline could be seen vaguely on the floor under a layer of silt and marine growth.

In the gloomy interior, there appeared the shapes of bunks in what must have been a stateroom. A brilliantly colored, long-nosed butterfly fish darted out the door, looking deceptively close to Julie's mask. Near its tail she could see its false eye. From the evening movies on Coral Island she had learned that this marking on the red and yellow fish was designed by nature to confuse predators as to which direction the fish was heading.

Farther down into the ruined ship, they swam through what appeared to be the crew's dormitory, and past a tangle of pipes and machinery which must have been the engine room. In the depths of the wreck, the old metal walls were softened by mossy marine growths, barnacle shells and undulating plants and sea worms, wherever the light penetrated. The closeness of the ship's interior became oppressive, and Julie gasped in a mouthful of dank water. She moved her hands from their usual finning position at her sides, and signaled to Les with her palms down, moving from side to side. Les responded by moving ahead of her and turning toward the sun-dappled water outside the ship.

Julie expelled the water from her mouth through her snorkel tube, but she couldn't retrieve her regular breathing pattern, and was relieved when they had pulled themselves back onto the rusty deck.

Les clambered down the cable to the boat, where he had left a waterproof pack containing a bottle of fresh water, which he brought to Julie. Julie lay on her stomach on the deck, A little sea water might have gone down her throat into her lungs. Les thumped her on her back, and that made her feel better. She sat up, leaning against a broken wall of the bridge. Les offered her a handful of dried fruit and nut mixture.

Julie shook out her hair, and Les produced a comb. He sat beside Julie and gently teased the tangles out of her hair so that it began to fluff out as much as it could after its immersion in salt water.

She looked out over the endless expanse of sea, hearing its rhythmic lapping along the wall of the old wreck. Les had his arm around her, her damp head resting against him, and she could feel his breathing, in tune with hers as well as with the gentle movements of the sea and the breeze that rippled the tattered remnants of a faded signal flag snagged against a piece of torn metal. Out here where the immensity of the sea surrounded them, Julie and Les seemed tiny specks in the universe, not much bigger than the hulking blue grouper that had finned its way beside them as they left the lower deck of the ship. She spoke of it to Les.

"Everything is cut down to size out here," he agreed, his gray eyes taking on a blue cast as he looked out to the distant horizon. "But it doesn't diminish your importance to me. My favorite undersea buddy."

They kissed. A magical bond seemed to exist between them, and when Les said, "I'll love you forever," this time Julie believed it.

"Even though we'll leave each other, you'll always be in my heart," she said.

"I told you before, I don't intend to become a memory, Julie," Les contradicted.

"I wish you didn't have to be," Julie said. Les was not practical enough to concede that their relationship was brief and temporary. Let him dream. He refused to face facts.

"We'd better go back," Julie said after they had explored the wreck and reef further. Les reluctantly agreed.

On the way back, he entertained her with stories of shipwrecks and salvage. Julie had never known anyone who was such good company, for he had a vast store of information to impart.

"It's illegal to take anything from a shipwreck," he told her, "but plenty of scavengers do. A legitimate salvage diver will get permission from the owner, or, if he's in the business, he may buy a wreck from its owner. Usually it's an insurance company that owns the wrecks, and they'll sell a crashed ship for practically nothing."

When they approached the far shore of Coral Island and Les pulled the little craft up on shore, Julie noticed that he expressed relief. "We made it!" he said in triumph. "The old motor isn't ready for the junk heap after all!"

"Did you think it might be?" Julie asked in surprise.

"It was more of a gamble than I should have taken with a valuable cargo," he said, and then a shadow crossed his sunny features.

"I had to have that last afternoon with you, Julie," he added, "no matter what."

Julie sensed a feeling of foreboding in his words, but he didn't elaborate.

"We'd better get to the pier, if that's where Dad and Jane will arrive. They'll be disappointed if we're not there to meet them. I hope they'll recognize me, since I'm looking like a worse wreck than the one we've been visiting."

"They'll see that you're much more tanned than you were when you came. And your dad should be pleased that you've learned a new skill, and learned it so well, if I may boast about my prize student."

When they inquired at the pier, Julie and Les found that their relatives had arrived about an hour before, and had been looking around the island for them. They hurried to Julie's cabin, and found Jane and Richard sitting on the porch.

"Where have you been?" Jane asked. "We've had the island combed for you, Les."

Julie could see Les's face pale under his skin, and an expression of unease cross his face.

"I just took Julie out for a little excursion. We weren't sure when you'd be arriving."

"Julie, your dad has the cabin right next door. Aren't they wonderful, tucked right into the forest? Richard and I have already been down to the beach. Have you ever seen such white sand?"

"Les, I can understand now why you didn't want to leave this to go to college. How can one leave a job in paradise?" he asked.

Julie ran next door to rap on her father's cabin.

"Julie," Mr. Blacker exclaimed, giving her a hug. "We thought you and Leslie had fallen off the pier and had been eaten by sharks. We had all Les's colleagues searching, and they said you'd just disappeared."

"We were out snorkeling, Dad, and Les showed me an old wrecked ship. We were having so much fun we forgot the time. Sorry I wasn't here to welcome you."

"You've enjoyed yourself on the island. That's the important thing."

"I have so much to talk to you about, Dad."

"We'll have the whole weekend. I was just changing into more casual clothes—taking off my necktie, that is, and wishing I had brought something besides my business suits."

"Daddy, we'll have to take you to the gift shop and buy you one of those T-shirts with a crocodile on it so you'll be properly dressed."

On the porch, Julie heard Kevin's voice addressing Les. "Here you are at last, Donaldson. You and your American friend quite gave us the slip today. Neil is asking for you over at headquarters."

"But my family just got in—I thought I had a free afternoon."

"Nevertheless, you'd better go over there and find out what he wants."

Julie went to the door of her father's room. She didn't like the sound of Kevin's voice. Something more was wrong. She hoped there wasn't more trouble connected with her afternoon's outing.

She watched Les walk down the trail with Kevin.

"I hope you don't mind that I have my possessions strung out all over the room," Jane said. "I couldn't wait to get to the beach. I'll put it to rights after a bit."

"Jane is renowned for scattering her belongings everywhere," Richard said, an affectionate smile playing about the corners of his mouth. "I follow her, picking up."

Jane gave him a playful swat. "Don't spread rumors, Richard. Julie, am I right? You've become one of Les's obsessions! I thought I saw it coming the evening you arrived in Australia. At our barbecue. Didn't I say so, Richard? I said to Richard, 'Just watch. Leslie is going to fall in love with Julie.'"

"That's exactly what she said," Richard confirmed.

"When he campaigned so hard to have you visit the island, there was no doubt about it. And just now, when you two came down the track, I knew I was right. I could tell he was head over heels."

Julie was speechless at Jane's brash discussion of her brother's private feelings.

"And when Leslie gets one of his obsessions, it's total," Jane ran on. "Remember, Richard, when his whole life hung on keeping this job? It was all we heard about in our family for days. Father and Leslie going round and round. Leslie never letting the subject drop until he had his way."

"He has a one-track mind. Once he's set on something, he'll go after it and won't let it go. The most persistent chap I've ever known," Richard chuckled.

"Yes, he's in love with you, and you're in for it," Jane concluded.

"But I'm only here for the week. It's just a temporary friendship." Julie was slightly offended by their directness.

"Leslie is very headstrong," Jane added. "He's been known to do desperate things to achieve his goal."

"Remember when he was younger and he wanted Tousle and your father said he couldn't keep him?"

"Tousle is our dog. You saw him. He was a shaggy Airedale pup," Jane said. "Les took him and ran away. Dad was frantic. They had the police out, and it was three days before they found Les and Tousle, sleeping in a barn on the outskirts of town."

"You two must have known one another for a long time," Julie said, eager to change the subject.

"Childhood sweethearts," Richard confirmed.

"He's been trailing me since we were twelve years old," Jane said. "I'm threatening to turn him in for a more up-to-date model."

"You'll never get away with it," Richard said.

"Let's go for a walk around the island before dinner. We need some exercise. That's what we came to the island for," Jane proposed.

"I ought to take a shower," Julie said. The old shirt she wore over her bathing suit was stiff with brine. "My hair is full of plankton."

"Don't worry about it," Jane said. "We might dunk you in the sea again on our way around the island."

"Well, okay. I'll shower when we get back." She went to her father's door. "Come on, Dad, we're going on a hike." When he appeared at the door, Julie looked with regret at the dress shoes and long trousers he was wearing. Julie persuaded him to go barefoot and roll up his pants.

Jane and Richard paced themselves ahead of Julie and her father, giving her a chance to converse with him.

"I've been longing to talk with you, Dad," she said.

"You only called me once this week," he reminded her. "When I didn't get an S.O.S. from you, I assumed you were adapting well to independence."

"I suppose I did. I've been busy all week. I'm just fascinated with what's under the sea. I've learned to live in a snorkel and fins. It's the most fun of anything I've done. Les says he'd like to take me down with an Aqualung, but he won't have time to give me the proper training. Anyway, when I get home I'd like to enroll in a scuba diving class."

"That would be an interesting new activity for you. And I take it that Les didn't cause you any trouble?"

"That's one of the things I wanted to talk to you about. You were right. He didn't get that much out of line, but I'm afraid I caused him trouble. You see, Dad, he has this weird idea that he's in love with me. He's always hanging around me when he should be working, neglecting the others he's supposed to be watching out for, getting himself in the doghouse. I've tried to convince him that after this weekend, he'll never see me again, and that he should cool it, but he won't. I like him a lot. In fact, he's the most terrific guy I've ever known, but he won't be sensible. I was wondering, since you're a guy, if you could suggest how I might turn him off. Jane says he gets these obsessions. He's very intense. Maybe you could talk some sense into him—impress him with the fact that we'll be moving on, and he should forget about me and take his job more seriously."

"I thought he took a shine to you, and I could see he was a hard-driving fellow who would develop deep attachments. But I'd say he was a pretty sensible young man to pick you out as the object of his affection. I'm surprised that you say he didn't trouble you with amorous advances, as intense as he is."

"He might have, if I hadn't been so scared of what could possibly happen. In fact, I thought about you and Mom and I pretended you were around waiting for me inside so I could put him off. I didn't encourage him. It takes two, you know, and as you predicted, Les has been raised like Harlan and I have, to respect another person's limits."

"I'm gratified to have been right about sending you out on your own, Julie. You can't imagine what it means to an aging father to see his daughter become mature enough to take care of herself."

"Aging! Come off it, Dad. But anyway, you gave me a good example of being a fantastic father. What other father would take his daughter on a trip like this? Anyway, it's not me that we have to worry about. It's Les. I care about him and I don't want him to get hurt. I only want him to come down to earth and be realistic. I can't understand what he sees in me, anyway. I'm not that glamorous. I'm a very ordinary person."

"Maybe you're not as ordinary as you think, and your modesty and lack of pretension may be an attraction to him. At any rate, being realistic and being in love are mutually exclusive for a volatile fellow like Les." Mr. Blacker chuckled. "Don't worry, Julie. The old sayings, 'time heals all wounds' and 'out of sight, out of mind,' will apply in his case. On Monday, we'll be flying down to Brisbane for a few days and then back home. He'll have no alternative but to forget about you."

"I hope so," Julie said dubiously. "Dad, I'm glad you're here for me to dump on."

"Dump away, and don't let it stop when we get back to Blossom Valley," he said. "I have a hunch you've been

keeping your feelings a secret from me for the last few
years."

Jane and Richard were waiting on the path for them, and
Julie took the lead then, showing the group the tree where
the herons nested, and other points of interest which Les had
shown her. "Les knows everything about this island, and
also about the reef and the bottom of the sea. You'll be very
impressed when you hear his spiel about it," Julie said.
"He's an unbelievable expert on everything."

Les met them briefly at tea. There was an air of tension
among the staff members. He seemed preoccupied and
moody, having little to say. Neil did not approach their
group, but busied himself with welcoming other visitors who
had just arrived to spend the weekend on Coral Island. Julie introduced Jane, Richard and her father to the remnants
of her snorkeling group who were still on the island—Al
Green and the brothers from Alice Springs. They all
watched the sunset from the terrace, and then Les disappeared with the staff while the others had dinner.

The routine was always the same on Coral Island. After
dinner, one could go to the movie, stroll around the beach
or browse in the library. The film this evening was the same
one Julie had seen the night she arrived on the island, but
she sat through it while her dad and the others became acquainted with the history of the reef. Another staff member ran the film, and Les was not even present.

"Les is making himself very scarce," Jane observed.
"Maybe he's avoiding us, Richard, thinking we came over
to the island just to pester him. We can get along without
him, can't we? Let's go for a moonlight stroll on the beach."

"I'll just stay here with Dad," Julie said, "and I'll see you
back in the cabin later."

Julie and her dad went back to the lounge and looked at
a small shell collection in the shelves. Julie questioned her

father about the people he had interviewed, the meetings he'd attended, and the progress of his article. They went back to the cabin and Les appeared briefly. They all had a Coke. Les conversed with Julie's dad in an uncharacteristically subdued manner. Shortly after Jane and Richard returned, he left. Julie wished they had been able to have a moment together so she could find out what was bothering him.

Jane chattered before they went to sleep about her friends and schoolmates in Cairns, and the next day they hiked again about the island. Julie went with her dad on a glass-bottom boat trip, for he didn't snorkel. Richard and Jane were old hands at it. They finned about Coral Island, although Les told them the sights weren't as spectacular there as they were farther away on the outer reef.

The weekend passed, and Julie became increasingly puzzled at Les's attitude. Had he ceased to express his affection because her father and his sister were present? Had he taken her advice and "cooled it," in view of the fact that they must part on Sunday, never to see one another again? A guy who claimed to love a girl ought at least to make the most of their last moments together. Moreover, he had been less than hospitable to his sister and her boyfriend. She didn't discuss Les further with her dad. Obviously, Les had decided to terminate their relationship without further ado or ceremony. Julie wondered if he would even bother to see them off when they departed from Coral Island on the Sunday catamaran.

When departure time approached, however, Les did appear at their cabins. He was not dressed in his Coral Island staff uniform, but in a plain navy blue T-shirt and shorts. There was not the usual sparkle of fun and mischief about his eyes, and his mouth was set in a grim line.

"I'll help you with your luggage down to the cart while you check out," he said.

"Leslie, you have hardly spent any time with us," Jane twitted him. "It's as if you wished we hadn't come. Surely your work doesn't extend to twenty-four hours a day."

Les wheeled around, his eyes suddenly blazing. "I'll be spending plenty of time with you from now on," he said, "because I'm going back with you. I'm no longer employed on Coral Island."

Chapter Twelve

On the trip back to Cairns, Les told them he'd been let go shortly after they had arrived on the island on Friday. First, there had been the complaint from Zelda, then the report by the rangers that Les's group had strayed into forbidden territory on the Cay. A spate of small transgressions such as getting a friend to put away the projector when that was Les's job had been added. "I found out that my snorkeling group had written a letter in my behalf to Neil—that must have been Julie's idea—but it didn't do any good. Neil thought I had instigated it myself. Then the final blow came when I took the boat out today. We're supposed to check it out. I was afraid I wouldn't get permission, and it was important to me to take Julie on an excursion on our last day alone together. I didn't think anyone would notice it was gone, but as luck would have it, Neil was going to have the engine overhauled, and when he went down to get it the boat was gone and my fate was sealed.

"I think he was always sorry he hired me anyway. He kept telling me I was just a holiday hire, for three months only, and he wanted more experienced, older people for the long-term. I finally wore him down, and I think he's resented me ever since."

"So you've been discharged! So that's why we haven't seen anything of you." Jane's mouth remained open in astonishment.

"What bloody bad luck!" Richard exclaimed.

"Why didn't you tell me?" Julie asked. "I could have gone to Neil and told him just how it was. That it was all my fault. Will would have apologized for invading the nesting colony. We could have told him again what a chronic complainer Zelda was. You didn't deserve to be fired. How could Neil let you go when you know everything about the reef? All that knowledge is going to be wasted now."

"I'm afraid our visit has interfered with your life, Leslie. We wouldn't have dreamed of intruding on your job," Mr. Blacker said.

"I know that, sir. Your visit did contribute, because I've become so enamored of your daughter that I wasn't able to concentrate on my work this week. I told Julie that I would endure anything for the privilege of her company, and that includes being sacked. As they say, every cloud has a silver lining, and now I'll be able to spend a few more hours with Julie."

"I knew it. I'm the one who predicted he'd fall in love with her. I think he engineered all those problems on purpose so he could come back with her," Jane said.

"It doesn't make sense," Mr. Blacker said, "because Julie is leaving tomorrow. I'm afraid you made a poor trade, Les, for you'll be left with nothing, and your father may regret his hospitality to us, since it's resulted in his having an unemployed son."

"Father never wanted Les to take that job permanently anyway," Jane said. "They had a fierce argument about it. Les never gives in. He argued night and day until Father was so tired of the quarrel that he surrendered. He was for Leslie enrolling in college."

"Perhaps you can do that now," Mr. Blacker said.

"It's too late for this term, sir." Les said. "I have a good scheme for the immediate days ahead, however. Instead of taking Julie to Brisbane with you tomorrow, you might leave her here with us. Jane and I could entertain her until you were ready to go back to America."

Mr. Blacker frowned forbiddingly and narrowed his eyes behind his wire-rimmed spectacles. "I'm afraid that won't do. We'll keep to our original plan."

"But Julie will be happier here. She'll probably be left alone while you transact your business."

"Since I gave up my traveling companion last week, I think I'm entitled to her company for the next one."

During this interchange, Julie was left on the sidelines, as though she had no say in her own fate. She could tell by the tone of her father's voice that the persuasive Les had met his match. Julie had argued with her father in the past, and the tone of his voice was meant to close the subject. She feared that her father was turning against Les, judging him to be an impractical fool.

"Yes, I'll have to go with Dad," Julie agreed. "After all, he brought me along so he wouldn't be lonely."

The catamaran skimmed over the waves toward the mainland, its loudspeaker system spewing out mood music. "Let's go downstairs awhile. I'll buy you a soda," Les said to Julie.

"We haven't had any time over the weekend," he said when they were away from the others. "I was trying to sort my thoughts out, going through everything that has happened. I'm afraid your father feels that I've made a mess of things, that I'm a failure with whom he'd rather you wouldn't associate. I hope you don't share his opinion."

"He doesn't have such an opinion, and neither do I. I've seen everything that happened, and I know you've been unfairly treated. I'm the one who made a mess of things for you."

"I'll never regret having this week with you. And I don't intend for it to end. We got your father to let you go to Coral Island. Now we'll persuade him to let you stay here."

"I doubt it. Dad can be an immovable object at times, and I can see that this is one of those times."

"Julie, I don't intend to let you go out of my life."

"I wish you hadn't let yourself get so deep into an attachment that has no future. Forget about me, Les."

"I have to find a way to keep you here."

"You're a dreamer, Les."

"You're more than a dream to me, Julie."

Al Green and the brothers from Alice Springs joined Julie and Les to reminisce about their week on Coral Island.

"It was great to swim with you guys," Julie said.

"Sorry that Will and I caused trouble for you on the Cay," Brian said.

"It wasn't your fault," Les told them, obviously impatient to have them move on so he could resume his conversation with Julie.

Jane and Richard clattered down the metal stairway. "Our parents are meeting us at the pier," Jane said. "They'll be surprised to see you, Les."

"The mainland is coming into view now," Richard said. "They'll probably be watching us dock."

"You and your father will come home with us for the evening, of course," Les said.

"It might cushion the blow of the news that Leslie has been sacked," Richard suggested.

Julie's father had joined them. "Julie and I will walk back to our hotel," Mr. Blacker said firmly. "We don't want to wear out our welcome."

"But sir," Les objected, "this is your last night in Cairns."

"We'll need to spend it packing for the next leg of our journey," Julie's father explained.

"But I had counted on being with Julie tonight," Les said in an aggrieved tone. "We can't just say goodbye at the pier. Mum and Father will have a proper send-off for you."

Les and Mr. Blacker argued until *The Dolphin* slipped into its berth on the pier.

"You want to come, don't you, Julie?" Jane asked.

"It's wonderful of you to invite us, but Dad is probably right. We should get organized for our trip tomorrow."

The passengers lined up to disembark from *The Dolphin*. Les squeezed in close to Julie and held her hand. They could see Mr. and Mrs. Donaldson smiling and waving on the pier. Their smiles turned to expressions of surprise when they noticed that Les accompanied the others.

"Mother, Father, I've been trying to convince the Blackers to come out with us for the evening," Les said.

"And while we're grateful, we've declined. We've imposed upon your hospitality enough, and we need to prepare for tomorrow's journey," Julie's dad said in an authoritative voice.

"We'd assumed you'd be coming with us to have dinner," Mrs. Donaldson urged.

"That's thoughtful, but Julie and I will have to go to our hotel."

"Father, it's their last night in Cairns. Persuade them to come," Les said. "I've been trying, without success."

"We weren't expecting you back, Leslie," his father said. "Did you get another leave so soon?"

"I'll explain later, Father."

Jane and Richard raised their eyebrows at one another and retired from the discussion.

"I can't tell you how much your assistance has meant to me," Julie's dad said to Les's father. He turned to Mrs. Donaldson. "And how pleasant it was to be entertained at your home and to know this fine son and daughter of yours. And it was a pleasure to meet you, too, Richard. Now, I'm going to let you get your clan home and give you a break from worrying about Julie and me."

"At least, we'll plan to take you to the airport tomorrow," Mr. Donaldson said.

"And keep you from your business for still another day? I wouldn't think about it after you've been so generous with your time for the past week," Julie's father said. "Julie and I will just grab a cab."

Les looked stricken, but Julie's father had a commanding air which indicated that he'd made up his mind and further discussion was useless. After a final exchange of formalities, the Donaldsons headed for their car, while Julie and her father, carrying their suitcases, walked the short distance down the Esplanade to their hotel.

"I hope you weren't too disappointed that we didn't spend the evening with your young friends," Mr. Blacker said. "But I felt that the Donaldsons would need to discuss Leslie's situation privately, and they'd be inhibited if we were along."

"Dad, I feel that I've ruined his life. Actually, I'm relieved that we're not going to their house. Les has lost that job that he was so crazy about, and it's my fault. The Donaldsons will wish they'd never seen me."

Julie went to the hotel laundry and washed out some of her things and her dad's, drying them while they went to dinner at a seafood restaurant down the Esplanade. It was restful to be alone with her dad, who entertained her with talk of his adventures during the past week.

They strolled under the trees on the Esplanade on their way back. The big ibis, doves and gulls that populated the scene by day were huddled asleep in clusters on the shore or in the trees. A few lights from boats and ships winked down the pier. When they reached their hotel rooms, the phone was ringing. Mr. Blacker answered, and handed the instrument to Julie.

"It's Les, Julie. I have to see you. I couldn't say a proper farewell to you with all the family there. I'm coming down right now."

"Well, okay, but just for a little while. Dad and I are doing some packing and laundry."

Les appeared in half an hour, looking distraught. Julie was waiting for him in the lobby.

"Let's go across the street, over on the Esplanade. I have some important things to tell you," he said.

"I had a lot of explaining to do to my father," he continued after they had crossed the street. "We have it all thrashed out. As Jane predicted, he wasn't too sorry that I'd lost my job on the island, since he was against it in the first place. I've pledged to start college next term, and meanwhile, of course, I'll be expected to work in my father's sugar business."

"I feel terrible, Les. I've turned your life upside down."

"You have changed everything. You're never going to be out of my thoughts. I want you to wear this all the time so you'll never forget me." Les took from around his neck a chain with a silver whale on it and placed it over Julie's head. "This had been my lucky charm for a long time and now it's going to be yours."

"I won't ever forget you, Les. I'll always wear it."

"I hope you never take it off." Les kissed her, giving her that giddy feeling.

"That wasn't a goodbye kiss, because I'm going to see you again, Julie," he said.

Julie argued with him again about being unrealistic, and after they'd talked a while, Julie's father happened to stroll past their bench and say that it was time for Julie to come in.

Les kissed her again, right in front of her father, and then, reluctant to leave her, got into his car which was parked near them on the Esplanade.

"Well, that's the end of that," Mr. Blacker said. They crossed the street to their hotel, Julie fingering Les's silver whale and feeling devastated.

Their clothes were all clean and neatly packed when the cab arrived the next day. Mr. Blacker had been pecking away on his portable typewriter all morning, and he slammed the cover on it just as Julie told him the taxi had arrived.

They were strapped into their airplane seats, ready to take off, when Julie thought she was confronted by an apparition. Her dad had the same sensation.

"Am I seeing things, or is that Leslie Donaldson coming down the aisle?" he said.

Les stopped beside their seats. "I hope you don't mind," he said. "I couldn't sleep at all last night. Thinking you'd be in Australia for a few more days, I couldn't stand not spending them with you. I had plenty of money saved up from my job, so I decided to go to Brisbane, too."

There were several passengers behind Les. The stewardess asked him to move on and quit blocking the way.

"What shall we do, Dad?" Julie asked in shocked surprise. "He once told me he was going to follow me back to the United States, and I'm afraid he meant it."

"That headstrong young man is going to have a date with me when we arrive in Brisbane," Mr. Blacker declared.

"Dad," Julie said. "You can't give him a bad time. Not after he's just got fired."

"Let me handle this," her dad said, looking very stern behind his wire-rimmed glasses.

Julie held the silver whale between her fingers and her heart gave a little flop.

"And Dad, would you not tell him anything that makes me seem like a child?"

It was a brief trip. When they arrived in Brisbane, Les muscled people aside pushing up the airplane aisle to be near Julie. "I hope you're not angry with me. It seemed the only thing to do."

"Do your parents know about this?" Mr. Blacker asked when they were out of the airplane and crossing to the airport.

"I left them a note."

Mr. Blacker clamped his mouth very tightly shut and strode to the baggage carousel. "Do you have a place to stay?" he asked Les.

"No sir, not yet. I thought I'd stay wherever you and Julie do. Here, let me get that." Mr. Blacker was reaching for his luggage on the carousel.

From the road leading to town, they had a view of the Brisbane River, a lazy, pale grayish blue waterway that ran into the sea.

"The houses in Brisbane are built on stilts, like those in Cairns," Julie remarked.

"Speaking about Cairns, we'll ring up your parents from the hotel," Mr. Blacker said, "just to let them know what's going on."

Les shared Julie's father's room at the hotel, and they had a long telephone conversation with the Donaldsons. One of the things they decided was that Les would attend some meetings with Julie's father about the sugar industry and report on it to his father.

After that, Mr. Blacker treated Les somewhat like a member of the family, as he might have treated Harlan if he were along. Sometimes when Mr. Blacker was writing, Julie and Les went exploring without him. They strolled in the botanical gardens, where poinsettias grew like trees, and tropical foliage similar to that in Cairns flourished. One day they went on an excursion boat to an offshore island. Les explained that it was not a reef island, for the Great Barrier Reef did not extend as far south as Brisbane, but ended at the Tropic of Capricorn. "The water south of that line isn't warm enough for coral to live," he explained.

"I'll never forget all the things you've taught me about the reef," Julie said.

"Let's never turn into memories to one another, Julie. Your father keeps lecturing me about how you still have a year of high school, and many years of college, and says, as you do, that we should look on this as a summer interlude. He keeps telling me about the various phases and turns people's lives take before they find their niche and settle down and discover what is important to them. I listened, but I know you'll never be an episode or a forgotten phase of my life, no matter how big an ocean is between us."

"Right now, while I'm with you, I feel the same way," Julie said, "but when we're on different paths, Dad may turn out to be right. I might fade out of your thoughts."

"Never."

Mr. Blacker saw to it that Les took a plane back to Cairns before he and Julie left for the United States. He was visibly relieved when they saw Les's flight winging northward. "Now we can be sure he's not going to stow away on our flight," he told Julie.

"What did you and Les talk about, Dad? I could hear your voices vibrating through the wall," Julie asked when they were en route back to the United States.

"Life—love—priorities. I tried to impress him with my superior experience, but I doubt if I influenced him much. Nobody could tell me anything when I was his age, either. I couldn't persuade him to stop loving my charming daughter and breaking his heart in the process. You don't encounter that kind of devotion often in life, Julie. He's a very fine and committed young man, and I hope you properly appreciate the fact that you knew him, even if it was in the wrong place at the wrong time."

"I do appreciate him. I'm afraid remembering him might hurt, Dad."

"If it does, I want you to come and, as you say, 'dump' on me, Julie."

"Dad, I'm glad you went through it with me. I used to think you weren't a person I could talk over such things with."

Harlan was at the San Francisco airport to meet them. Although Julie and her dad were groggy from the long, grueling trip across the Pacific Ocean, they answered all of Harlan's eager questions.

"I took a lot of pictures. You'll see everything when I get them developed," Julie said. When they pulled up at the Blackers' home, it looked smaller than Julie remembered. Mrs. Blacker ran down the front walk to embrace them.

"A very strange thing happened a while ago," she said. "There was an overseas call for Julie. I said she was due home at any moment, and the operator said she'd call back."

Julie looked at her dad, rolling her eyes heavenward, and her dad grinned and winked at her.

The Blackers were no sooner in the house than the phone rang again. Harlan ran for it. "It's that overseas operator. Julie. Quick." Everyone stood around listening, so Julie went into the closet. The line crackled with static. "Julie, Les. I've been so impatient for you to get home that I've called twice. I wanted to be the first one to welcome you home."

"Les, you nut. It must cost you a fortune to telephone me from Australia."

"No price is too high to pay for hearing your voice."

Les told her he'd start working in his father's sugar mill on Monday, and that he was preparing his college application. He asked Julie to send him a picture of herself, and she promised to send him copies of snapshots she'd taken on Coral Island.

"I'm going to write you a letter as soon as we're through talking," Les said.

"I'll write to you after I get some sleep."

"Keep me in your dreams."

Julie gave Harlan a Great Barrier Reef T-shirt, and she had a gift of a coral necklace for her mother. The next day she got together with her friend, Kim. Kim's present was a stuffed white cockatoo that hung from a string and flapped its wings.

"Mike Washburn is back in town," Kim said.

"Oh?" Julie didn't feel any emotion at the news.

"Are you going to start up with him again?"

Julie shrugged. "I don't know. Maybe, if he asks me, just for old times' sake. But I think I'll try to get acquainted with some other guys this year. Mike was sort of a phase, you know, that you outgrow. As you go through life, you meet other people. For instance—" Julie had taken her film to a quickie print shop, and she showed Kim a snapshot of Les on board *The Dolphin*, his long blond hair shining against the dazzling sea.

"Wow, who is this?" Kim asked.

Before Julie could answer, the phone rang, and it was the overseas operator again.

Kim heard Julie say, "Les Donaldson, are you out of your mind? I just talked to you yesterday!"

"You're never out of my mind, Julie, so I have to make sure I'm still in yours."

"Believe it, you are."

"I've started a kitty to buy myself a ticket to America. Your father invited me to come over and visit."

"You're using up all your travel money calling me. Can't you be practical, Les?"

"Haven't you learned by now that where you're concerned, practicality isn't one of my assets?"

After they hung up, Kim asked in awe: "That wasn't the smashing guy you met in Australia, was it?"

"The same. He's this very weird unpredictable guy I don't know what to do about."

"I should have a problem like that," Kim said, looking at Les's picture. "A phone call from Australia! That's what I call romantic!"

"Dad," Julie said that evening when her father arrived home. "I have a problem I'd like your advice on. It's Les. He's telephoning me every day. It must be costing him his total savings. What shall I do?"

"Put me on the next time he calls. Let me give him a piece of my mind about this ridiculous extravagance," he said. Then he smiled. "You know, Julie, I kind of miss that impetuous bloke."

"I miss him, too, Dad." A tear squeezed out of Julie's eye and splashed on the silver whale.

QUANTITY	BOOK #	ISBN #	TITLE	AUTHOR	PRICE
☐	129	06129-3	The Ghost of Gamma Rho	Elaine Harper	$1.95
☐	130	06130-7	Nightshade	Jesse Osborne	1.95
☐	131	06131-5	Waiting for Amanda	Cheryl Zach	1.95
☐	132	06132-3	The Candy Papers	Helen Cavanagh	1.95
☐	133	06133-1	Manhattan Melody	Marilyn Youngblood	1.95
☐	134	06134-X	Killebrew's Daughter	Janice Harrell	1.95
☐	135	06135-8	Bid for Romance	Dorothy Francis	1.95
☐	136	06136-6	The Shadow Knows	Becky Stewart	1.95
☐	137	06137-4	Lover's Lake	Elaine Harper	1.95
☐	138	06138-2	In the Money	Beverly Sommers	1.95
☐	139	06139-0	Breaking Away	Josephine Wunsch	1.95
☐	140	06140-4	What I Know About Boys	McClure Jones	1.95
☐	141	06141-2	I Love You More Than Chocolate	Frances Hurley Grimes	1.95
☐	142	06142-0	The Wilder Special	Rose Bayner	1.95
☐	143	06143-9	Hungarian Rhapsody	Marilyn Youngblood	1.95
☐	144	06144-7	Country Boy	Joyce McGill	1.95
☐	145	06145-5	Janine	Elaine Harper	1.95
☐	146	06146-3	Call Back Yesterday	Doreen Owens Malek	1.95
☐	147	06147-1	Why Me?	Beverly Sommers	1.95
☐	149	06149-8	Off the Hook	Rose Bayner	1.95
☐	150	06150-1	The Heartbreak of Haltom High	Dawn Kingsbury	1.95
☐	151	06151-X	Against the Odds	Andrea Marshall	1.95
☐	152	06152-8	On the Road Again	Miriam Morton	1.95
☐	159	06159-5	Sugar 'n' Spice	Janice Harrell	1.95
☐	160	06160-9	The Other Langley Girl	Joyce McGill	1.95

Your Order Total $\underline{\hspace{3cm}}$

☐ (Minimum 2 Book Order)
New York and Arizona residents
add appropriate sales tax $\underline{\hspace{3cm}}$

Postage and Handling   .75

I enclose $\underline{\hspace{3cm}}$

Name_____

Address_____

City_____

State/Prov._____ Zip/Postal Code_____

COMING
NEXT MONTH

MAYHEM AND MAGIC Nicole Hart
A Hart Mystery!

When May took on a summer job, she found herself
involved in a murder attempt. Fortunately she had
busybody Eustice and a new attractive boyfriend to help
her crack the case.

SOAP OPERA Joyce McGill

Leslie found herself in hot water when she deceived her
parents and her new boyfriend in order to get a job as a
shampoo girl in a beauty parlor. What would she do when
her bubble burst?

PLAYING HOUSE Jean Simon

Now that she was juggling two boyfriends, Marcy should
have been having a blast. Yet somehow things had gone
awry. How could she have ever thought guys so great?

HUNTER'S MOON Brenda Cole

When Adam showed up with a starved stray at her father's
kennels, Katie thought that he was the most attractive boy
she'd ever seen. Unfortunately, she was not the first to
have felt this way.

AVAILABLE THIS MONTH: